Torquere Press Novels

The Broken Road
TOP SHELF
An imprint of Torquere Press Publishers
PO Box 2545
Round Rock, TX 78680
Copyright © 2006 by Sean Michael
Cover illustration by Pluto
Published with permission
ISBN: 1-934166-39-1, 978-1-934166-39-0
www.torquerepress.com
First Torquere Press Printing: December 2006
Printed in the USA

# Prologue

The sun was setting by the time Ardie came in out of the fields. Fall was riding him hard this year, bearing down on him with the promise of frost, and he was down two helpers. Luke was off at college on a scholarship, making them all damn proud. Agnes was knocked up again, making him not so proud.

Kid number four and she still didn't have a man willing to step up and *be* a man. Mabel had just sighed when Aggie'd told them and muttered something about how one more baby wasn't going to make that much of a difference anyway.

Ardie just wondered how long a man without a wife or a child of his own was going to be kept up nights by babies needing bottles and diapers changed and rocking back to sleep. Hell, he didn't mind really, he was just tired was all, and he still had the back forty to bring in or they'd be short on feed this winter.

Alice and Donny and little Robbie were sitting on the porch when he came up, all but Robbie working on their homework.

"Bu-Pa, Bu-Pa, lookit wha' I made." Robbie held out a scrap of construction paper with a brown blob on it.

"Well, look at that. Is it Trigger?" he asked, the old hound dog woofing at the sound of his name, tail thumping on the weatherworn wood.

"It is! It is! See, Alli? Told-u Bu-Pa'd *know*."

"Leave Bu-Pa alone now, kids," murmured Mabel from the door. "He's had a long day and wants his dinner."

He shared a tired smile with his sister. Her day had likely started before his and was damn near as physical now that she was running that shop, cooking up a storm all day.

"I've got a plate warming in the oven for you. You want it out here?"

He nodded and settled in the old rocker, getting kisses from the kids before they moved on inside. Damn, he felt like a grandfather some days, like he was 82 instead of 32.

A breeze blew up, surprisingly warm for October, and he raised his face to it, eyes catching sight of a damned pretty sunset, clouds all pink and dusky purple fading to dark, dark blue. That breeze promised a few more days grace to get his crops in. Maybe Mother Nature was going to give him a break for a change.

He was still enjoying her show in the sky when Mabel brought him a plate of roast beef with new potatoes and peas, salad and a buttered roll on the side. She had a bottle of beer for him, too. "You wanting a mug?"

He shook his head. "This'll do me, thanks."

She nodded and went back in to herd the kids, and he dug in, eating hearty.

By the time he was done, the sun was nearly set and he was rocking, beer half drunk, him half asleep and dreaming about being thirteen again and begging his Daddy to let him and West Silvers help in the fields instead of going to school.

He'd already been nearly a head taller than West, then, getting his growth in early. West had been his best friend and the first boy he'd ever loved. Hell, the only boy.

Not that he'd ever said. Only Mabel ever knew, her warm blue eyes seeing everything. They always had. And she'd only ever asked him about it once, just after West had left that first time. Asked why he hadn't said anything to make West stay.

Well, by then he was 17 and head of the family, three younger siblings to care for, a farm to run. No way he'd ask West to stay with him and bury his talent, his potential, in the dusty ground.

His reverie was broken by Mabel coming out with the portable. "It's for you, Ardie."

"Thanks." He gave her a smile and took the phone. "Hello?"

It took a bit for someone to answer, the voice rough and husky. "Ard? Ard, that you?"

"West?" He'd barely recognized the voice, it was so rough. He sat up, frowning. "What's wrong?"

"I... I need you. Can you come?"

"Where?" he asked. He'd call Jim and ask him to bring in the back forty if he was gone more than a day or two.

"Presbyterian Hospital. Room 412. I'll be in here for another five days, give or take..."

"Up in Seattle?" Shit, the hospital. There was a call you never wanted. He kept his questions to himself, though, West would explain when he got there. And there was no question he'd go.

"Yeah. I'll buy the ticket. I... I just need you, Ard. Please."

"Don't worry yourself. I'll drive down to the city today and take the first flight out they got. Hold on, West, I'm coming."

"Thank you. I'm sorry, Ard. I am."

"Hey now, that's what best friends are for, right?" He cleared his throat. "You gonna be all right?"

"I hope so."

"You sit tight, and I'll be there this time tomorrow. You can tell me all about it." He wanted to talk now, but figured the call was costing West a pretty penny. "K?"

"Okay. I'll see you tomorrow. Thank you, Ardie." He heard West sigh. "I appreciate it."

"Anytime, West." And he meant it, too.

He hung up the phone and headed in to pack some clothes, let Mabel and Aggie know where he was going, make a few calls to make sure the critters and crops would get taken care of.

# Chapter One

First day of school was always a bit scary, but Ardie didn't show it. He was in second grade this year. A big boy -- not one of the babies who clung to their mommas and cried when they got off the bus. Nope. Not him.

He kicked a stone around the yard, waiting on the bell to ring, nodding to Jimmie Rusk and Brad Watson. They were in the fourth grade, but they were his neighbors, so he knew 'em, and it made him feel all growed up to say hey.

The girls were all sitting together by the swings, talking and giggling. Silly girls.

There was a bit of a scuffle over in the corner by the wall and he kicked his stone over that way, curious.

Henry Martin was pushing around some little new boy wearing brand-new jeans and big ole ugly horn-rimmed glasses who looked like he was pushing right back. Henry Martin was a bully, picking on kids smaller and younger than him. Ardie wasn't scared of him, though; Ardie was almost as big as Henry and had learned how to throw a punch over the summer.

"Lemme be! I ain't hurt you none!" The little boy was fixing to cry.

Ardie frowned. Now that wasn't right. He pushed his way into the circle of kids watching. "You leave him be, Henry Martin."

Henry turned, face all red. "This ain't your business, Ardie-Pardie."

His own face got red from the name-calling, but he wasn't gonna back down because of that. "Call me what you want, I'm not gonna let you keep bullying him just because he's new. He ain't never done nothing to you."

The new boy picked up a book bag, swinging it in a wide circle and whacking Henry square in the back, knocking him flat. "C'mon! Run."

Ardie felt his eyes go wide, but he wasn't stupid, and he took off after the new kid, getting the hell out of there before Henry could get back up and retaliate.

They ran around to the side of the school, near the basketball hoop where the big kids stayed. "Th...thanks. Thanks. Is... is he always mean?"

Ardie nodded. "Pretty much." He held out his hand, like a big boy. "I'm Ardie."

"Ardie? That's a weird name. Mine is, too. I'm West."

Ardie shuffled his feet. "Real name's Maynard," he whispered, figuring if he and West had an enemy in common, he was safe sharing his name.

He got a grin. "Mine's Westonbury like my Pa-paw's, but don't tell no one."

He chuckled and nodded. "Well, I'll keep your secret if you keep mine." He spit in his hand and offered it to West. A spit-shake was solemn.

"'Kay." West spit, too, and they shook on it, both wiping their hands on their jeans. "What grade are you in?"

"Two. You?"

"Second, too. Momma says there's only one teacher, so we'll be in the same class, huh?"

He nodded and grinned. "Yeah. Cool. Wanna be best friends for life?" Until last winter he'd thought Bobby Slowicki was his best friend for life, but Bobby and his folks had left before Easter, moving to the city.

"Okay, cool. I got two cupcakes for lunch. You could have one." Those glasses were pushed up and he got a grin.

"Cupcakes? Awesome." He grinned back. "You can have half my apple -- if I don't eat it all, Momma'll yell."

"Oh, I like apples. What kinda sandwich do you get?"

"Probably ham or cheese. Wanna go halfsies?"

"Sure. I got peanut butter and banana." The bell rang and West jumped a little. "Is that mean boy in our grade?"

"Oh, that sounds good. And nope. Fourth. He only picks on kids smaller than him." He showed West where they were supposed to line up and go in, the little kids getting to go in first. "You just follow me, and sit next to me, okay?"

"Okay. Cool. Thanks, Ardie. I 'preciate it."

"That's what friends are for, right?" He gave West a grin. He had a feeling they were gonna be really good best friends.

*\*\*\**

"Okay, Ardie. Ready or not, here I come!" West started looking in the barn. Ardie wasn't as good at hiding as he was, but this was Ardie's *home*, so he knew all the best hidey-holes.

Him and Ardie were getting to spend a *whole* week together while Momma and Daddy were going on vacation.

A whole week.

It was so cool.

He was about to give up on the barn when he heard the softest giggle. It sounded like it came from one of the stalls. He grinned, started walking slower, listening. The giggle cut off, but he thought he heard Ardie shifting. Definitely in the first stall, the one with all the bales of straw.

He slid around the side and pounced, jumping on Ardie where he was hiding in the straw. "Gotcha!"

Ardie shouted and squealed, rolling with him. "Now I've got you!"

They laughed so hard he thought he might puke. "Uncle! Uncle!"

Ardie stood and helped him up. "How did you know where I was? I thought for sure you missed me."

"I heard you. You laughed."

"Oh, man!" Ardie shook his head.

He leaned against the wall, grinned. "You gonna go out for football, you think?"

"I will, if Poppa'll sign. He says I've got to prove I can still do my chores and homework and stuff. You gonna? You're not big, but you're *fast*, West. You'd make a good quarterback."

"Nope. Gonna play baseball. Momma says my glasses'll get broke in football." He really thought it was that Momma thought he'd get hurt, but it wasn't like he could *argue*. You went to hell for arguing with your momma, preacher said so.

"Oh." Ardie looked at the ground, kicking at the straw, shoulders slouched. "I'm way better at football than baseball. No way Poppa'll let me do both."

"Well, I'll come to your games if you come to mine." That sounded real fair.

And it got him one of Ardie's grins. "You got a deal."

"Cool." He grinned. "What do you think your mom's gonna make for supper?"

"Chicken fried steak and fried potatoes." It was his favorite and he knew Ardie knew that. "There's even chocolate coconut cake for dessert."

"Oh, wow! For real? Your momma's the greatest." At least second to his own momma, anyway.

Ardie grinned and nodded. "Yep. She is. Hey! You wanna go fishing? The creek's high this summer. I reckon there's some good ones in there."

"Oh, yeah. That'd be cool. We gonna use worms or bacon?"

"I dug up some nightcrawlers this morning. Got 'em in the shed so the sun doesn't dry 'em out. Come on." Ardie's arm went around his shoulders as they headed to the shed.

It was going to be the best week *ever*.

\*\*\*

Ardie wasn't going to cry because boys didn't. Especially boys in the fifth grade. But it wasn't fair, it so totally wasn't.

He'd gotten kicked off the football team for missing too many practices. It wasn't his fault, though -- Poppa *needed* his help on the farm bringing crops in. If they didn't get them all in, and the cattle or pigs went hungry, then they could lose the farm, or not get to eat themselves. It wasn't like he'd goofed off or anything.

Coach just wasn't being fair.

Ardie was too mad to get on the bus home, so he just started walking, feet kicking at the dirt as he went. And he was very definitely *not* crying.

"Ardie? Ardie? You okay?" West's voice sounded close behind him, skinny legs carrying him so fast.

He turned to look at West and shook his head. "Got kicked off football."

"What for? You're good!" West's voice was outraged, furious.

He smiled. West was the best friend ever. Then he remembered and he stopped smiling and he sighed. "I missed too many practices."

"Well, make your daddy talk to the coach, explain. It ain't your fault, Ard."

"*I* explained it to Coach, and he said he understood I had chores to do, but if I couldn't put the football first, I couldn't play." And he was gonna cry now, with West being nice to him.

"Yeah, but you know Coach Johnson's a prick, Ardie. Your dad'll fix him up right."

"I don't know, West." He stepped a little closer and spoke soft. "I don't think he was too happy with the time football was taking from me helping out."

West sighed, shook his head. "You work all the time, Ardie. It ain't fair."

He nodded. "I know. But I'm not smart like you, and my homework already takes up a couple hours a day just to keep up, and then chores, and football, and... well, there's not enough time in the day it seems. I hardly never see you anymore 'cept in school."

"Well, I'll come and help you. Momma won't mind."

"You will?" He beamed at West. "That would be so great. Maybe if I got my grades up Poppa'd let me try out again and talk to Coach for me."

"No sweat. I'll even read your lessons to you while you're working. That'll save time." Oh, man. West was the best friend ever.

"You sure your Momma won't mind?" He didn't want to get West into trouble.

"Momma never minds."

Ardie nodded. West's Momma never seemed to mind enough, and his minded too much. "You didn't have to walk all the way home with me, you know." They still had a couple miles to go before they got to the farm. Poppa'd drive West home after supper, though, he always did.

"I got nothing else to do. Oh!" West grinned, bounced. "I bought a chocolate bar and two came out. That's why I came looking for you."

"No way! What kind?" He could almost bounce for chocolate himself. And it was a nice afternoon, the sun warm and the breeze kind of nice, making what was left of the grain in the fields whisper. And with West to walk with it wasn't so bad at all.

"Three Musketeers." One bar was handed over, West all grins.

"Oh. Those are my favorites." He beamed and opened the bar. "Thanks, West. You're the best."

"No problem. Glad I caught you."

He nodded, steps picking up a little as he ate the treat. "Me, too."

Suddenly, the worst day ever? Still wasn't great, but he was going to make it through it without crying.

***

West took off down the road, legs just pumping, hearing the jeers and hollers fading behind him, the rocks hitting less and less often. Damn that Henry asshole and all his asshole friends anyway.

He headed for Main Street, knowing that the boys wouldn't follow them down there, that the old biddies that worked and shopped down there would fuss and chatter if they did. He had a five in his pocket and he was hoping to get a Coke and a bag of chips and then make the walk to Ard's house.

First, though? He was going to sit a spell.

Ardie's Poppa's truck went by and then pulled up halfway down the road, Ardie jumping out of the passenger seat and trotting up to him. "Hey, West! What'cha doing sitting on the curb?"

"Restin'. Henry and them jumped me outside the basketball court." He grinned up. "I was coming to see you."

Ardie growled. "They still there? I'll go back with you and beat his sorry ass up."

"There's lots of 'em and they're throwing rocks, Ard." West rolled his eyes, sighed. "I got money. You want a soda?"

Ardie sighed and nodded. "It ain't right, though, West. A bunch of 'em picking on one." Ardie held out a hand and helped him up.

"Yeah, well... lots of sh... stuff ain't right. Let's get a drink 'fore your daddy's done."

Ardie nodded. "Cool. And you can ride home with us." Ardie was quiet a minute. "Did you see there's a dance for middle school graduation?"

"Yeah. You asking someone?" West wasn't going with anyone, so there wasn't anyone to ask.

Ardie shook his head and shoved his hands in his pockets. "I don't..." he sighed. "Momma says I'm just a late bloomer."

"Yeah. You wanna have a sleepover instead? I can bring my Atari."

Ardie beamed at him. "Hell, yeah! I mean heck, yeah."

"Cool. That sounds way cooler than watching Annie Lester make eyes at you." He winked, hurried before Ard popped him.

"She does not!" Ardie called after him, catching up with him as they went into the diner. "Well, I don't make 'em back, anyway."

"Yeah, well, she's got scary teeth -- all braces and retainers and stuff."

Ardie nodded. "Yeah. Momma keeps saying she'll look real pretty when she's all grown up, and be a real good catch, but I don't think I want to catch her. Even if she was all prettied up. I'm never getting married."

"No? Me neither, though Mom says I'll change my mind one day and fall in love." He rolled his eyes. Stupid girl stuff.

"I'm never gonna fall in love. You're my best friend, West. That's good enough for me."

Ardie and him sat at the counter. "You got enough for us to have some fries, too, West?"

"Yup." He ordered two Cokes and a large portion of fries, legs just swinging. "Did you do good on the math test?"

"I did okay. C+. I know it, too, you explained it real good. I just didn't finish everything. There's never enough time in the tests."

"Yeah. You have to always hurry-hurry." 'Course he didn't, really. The tests were easy, especially after helping Ard.

Ardie nodded. "So I wind up not finishing half or making mistakes." His friend shrugged. "I'm not smart like you."

"You're plenty smart. You do stuff all the time at home I can't." Daddy said all the time that there was different kinds of smarts.

"Farming just comes natural to me." Ardie looked pleased, though, that West thought he was smart.

"Yeah, it's all in your bones." Of course, that made him a drunk and a trucker, but still...

"Nah, you need muscles." Ardie looked at him sideways, mouth twitching.

He popped Ard's arm. "I got muscles! They're just *little* muscles."

Ardie laughed, rubbing his arm like it had really hurt. "Ow!" Oh, Ardie's eyes just danced when he was laughing. They laughed until the waitress brought their Cokes, then they settled back down, just giggling every now and again.

Ardie sucked down half of his before saying softly. "Momma's gonna have another baby. Man, I hope it's a brother this time."

"Yeah? That would be cool. When?" He didn't have any brothers or sisters; didn't want any either.

"End of summer. Oh! And Poppa said I could have rabbits this summer when school's out. You could help me and we'll share the money."

"Yeah? Where you gonna put 'em?" The fries came out and they ketchupped and salted them.

"Poppa said if I clear out the shed, it's mine. And if the rabbits do well, I can take over the care of the chickens. That's eggs as well as chicks and broilers. Will you help me, West?"

"Sure, 'cept... Man, that rooster's *mean*." He grinned. "Just think, three years we'll get our licenses, and we can drive over whenever."

"That'll be great," murmured Ardie, stuffing his face with fries. "You think I can get ten in at once?"

"Only if you got ketchup on 'em to slick 'em up." Dork.

"I bet I can do it without the ketchup."

Ardie picked up ten, counting carefully and then gave him a grin and opened wide, shoving them all in.

"Trod chu," mumbled Ardie around his mouthful.

"Don't sneeze or nothing." He chuckled, stealing a real crispy one.

Ardie gave him a *look*, mouth muscles tightening and he could see Ardie was trying hard not to laugh.

"If you laugh and spew? You'll get ketchup everywhere, and I'll scream, and it'll look like you killed me." Teasing Ardie was the most fun.

Ardie poked a finger at him, eyes going so big, free hand going in front of his mouth as Ardie started to giggle audibly.

"Don't! Chew! Chew, Ardie! Chew!"

Ardie chewed once or twice and then swallowed hard, almost choking as he laughed hard.

Oh, man. Ardie was the most fun *ever*.

Ardie's laughter slowed, along with his choking. "You're crazy, West."

"Yep. Crazy like a fox!" The words had them both laughing again.

They finished up the fries and their Cokes. "Come on, West. Best not make my Poppa come look for us."

"I'm right behind you." He grabbed his book bag and grinned. "Let's go."

Ardie led the way, heading right toward the feed store. "You wanna sleepover tonight?"

"Sure. Your folks don't mind?"

"You're practically family, West. 'Sides, if it wasn't for you I'd be failing school." They turned a corner and saw Ardie's Poppa loading up the back of the truck. Ardie picked up speed.

"Afternoon, Mr. Bodine." He hurried along, too, so he could help lift the salt licks into the bed.

Ardie's Poppa nodded to him, grunting approval as he and Ardie started helping. "Didn't think you were gonna make it."

"We were just talking, Poppa."

West nodded, hauling the blocks up. "You got lots of stuff today."

"Yep. Brought a bunch of pigs in to slaughter on Wednesday. Got a good price for 'em, too. You boys want to stop at Hardigan's? He's got a bull I wouldn't mind getting a look at, and you can see if his rabbits are ready for sale yet."

Ardie's eyes lit up. "Yeah? We could get them now?"

"Well, I reckon the two of you could get that shed cleaned out today if you put your backs into it."

Ardie nodded. "Yes, sir, we sure could. Couldn't we, West?"

West nodded. "Yessir. I'll help." He'd do damned near anything to keep Ard all grinning.

Ardie was bouncing and grinning all right, picking up speed as he helped load up the truck. "Oh, boy! Between the rabbits and the chickens, I bet we could save up enough for a car of our own by the time we're old enough to drive, West. Wouldn't that be something?"

"Oh, that would be cool. My daddy has a friend who owns a car lot. Good deals."

"Great!"

They climbed into the truck, Ardie sitting in the middle and just beaming away at him, a grin on Mr. Bodine's face. "You boys got it all planned out, don't you."

"Ard's a good planner; I just go along with the good ideas." He grinned, winked as Arb nudged his knee.

Ard gave him a hug and then resumed his bouncing. "It's gonna be a *great* summer."

West nodded. "The best. You just watch."
\*\*\*

Ardie loved summer.

Him and West would work hard all morning and then they'd grab some sandwiches and a couple apples and head off on their bikes. They usually went out to the creek at the far end of the farm and splashed and ate and just baked in the bright, hot sunlight.

He was lying in the sun, chewing on a piece of straw, feeling hot and lazy, like a lizard on a rock.

West was sitting and reading some book about spaceships and robots, all tanned and skinny, legs folded up under him.

Ardie didn't think life could possibly get any better than this. He really didn't.

He watched his friend read for a bit and then closed his eyes again and just soaked.

He was almost asleep, so he completely missed West picking up the bucket of water until the first splash of cold water hit him. He squealed like a girl, the water seeming like ice on his sun-baked skin. He jumped up and grabbed West around the waist, wrestling him toward the creek. West squealed, fighting him, twisting and turning in his arms.

He was a lot bigger than West now, though, stronger from working on the farm and playing football, and slowly but surely, they got closer and closer to the creek and its cool, fresh water.

"Uncle! Come on, now, Ard! You looked hot. I was being *friendly*!"

He chuckled. "Well, I'm just being friendly back, West."

"But..." West reached out, started tickling him.

"Oh! Oh, *cheater*!" He tried to shield his sides and wrestle West the rest of the way to the water at the same time.

For a skinny kid, West could sure struggle.

By the time he got West at the water's edge he was breathless, and when he tried to dump West in, he wound up going down, too, West breaking his fall as the water splashed up around them.

West groaned, still laughing a little. "Get *off,* you heavy footballing thing!"

He was laughing, too, and he kind of bounced on West. "Not until you say 'uncle' and mean it!"

"Not gonna!" West's fingers found his ribs.

Man, West knew *exactly* where he was ticklish, making him twist and writhe and slip right off West into deeper water.

"Ha!" West stood, hips wagging, cheering over him.

He cupped his hand and sent a pile of water up toward West, his aim a little shoddy because of all the laughing. Still, he managed to get West pretty damned wet, sputtering and wiping his face.

They climbed out of the creek bed together, soaked and laughing, the sun keeping them from being cold.

"You're a big dork, Ard." West winked over, eyes twinkling.

"You're a bigger one." Well. Probably not, but you didn't just accept getting called a dork. Even by your best friend.

"Maybe a faster one..." West started laughing, tossing water at him.

He laughed and tackled West again and they rolled in the dust together.

"Oh, we're gross." West wrinkled his nose, shook his head. "Gross, gross, gross."

He nodded. "Better go for a swim, West."

"Ard... There's critters in the pond..."

"Oh, you aren't scared are you? Of getting bit?"

He giggled and pulled off his T-shirt. "Think a fish is going to bite your weiner?"

"It *could*!" West blushed, shook his head. "And I ain't scared."

"Prove it!" He stripped right down and waded in, trying not to worry on it now that West had mentioned it. He hadn't even thought of it before.

West stripped down, too, making enough splashes and noise as he got hip deep to scare *anything* off. Ardie laughed, but he was looking, too. Not staring or nothing, but noticing the long, thin limbs, the way West's tan cut off where his shorts usually were.

Then West splashed a big ole bunch of water in his eyes and he sputtered, West's laugh filling the air. Oh, the fight was on then, the two of them splashing and laughing and hollering. By the time it was all over, they were soaked, panting, both of them a mess.

They dragged themselves back on the bank. "Oh, man, Momma's gonna yell."

"We'll walk slow and be dry... Or we could go to my house. My mom won't care."

"Yeah? We could play some Atari. I'll call my mom and tell her where we are when we get there." He'd done all his chores. It should be okay.

"Cool. We'll order pizza." West's mom didn't cook. Ever.

"Cool. I like pizza." And he only got stuff like that with West. "Don't forget your book."

"Oh, yeah. Thanks." West grabbed the book, marking his page. "Pepperonis and hamburger?"

"Bacon, too." He put his sneakers back on and, ignoring the squelching, headed off with West.

Yeah. Summer rocked.

# Chapter Two

West didn't want to go to Ardie's house. At all.

Not even a little.

He'd never known anybody whose dad died, and yeah, okay, he wasn't a baby, but he didn't know what to say to Ardie.

His mom had hugged him and given him a big plate of store-bought brownies and put his butt in the car. "You have to go, baby. You *have* to. Ardie's your best friend."

"I won't know what to say."

"Start with I'm sorry and go from there." She smiled at him, pulled into the long driveway. "He's still Ardie, West. He's still your friend."

They got out of the car, and Agnes, Ardie's ten year old sister, came down from the porch, eyes big and round. "He's in the shed with the rabbits," she whispered to West.

West handed her the brownies. "'Kay. I'll go see him."

It was the longest walk *ever*.

"Ard? You here?"

"West?" Ardie came from the back of the shed, his face streaked. "I been waiting for you to come."

"Yeah. I didn't know if I should. You..." You okay was what he wanted to say, but he knew Ardie wasn't okay. "I missed you at school."

"I missed you, too." Ardie just looked so sad, none of the usual easy going smile on him.

"Are y'all okay? Is there anything I can do?"

"I..." Ardie shook his head and moved closer. "I'm tired."

"I'm sorry, Ardie. Real sorry." He didn't know what to do. At all.

Ardie leaned forward and leaned his head on West's shoulder. "Me, too." The words were broken, half spoken.

He reached up, hugged Ardie hard. "It'll be okay, you'll see. I'll help. Everybody'll help."

Ardie nodded and sobbed, hands sliding around his waist, his friend just holding on.

"I'll help, Ardie. I promise." His eyes got all teary, too, but he just patted and hugged and tried not to wig out.

"I just want it to be last week, West. I don't want this to be real."

He nodded. "Yeah. Yeah, me, too. Your momma okay?"

"I don't know. She hasn't said a word." Ardie let him go and grabbed his hand, tugging him over to the corner to sit in the straw. "There a lot of people out there still?"

"Uh-huh. Some. Mom says I can stay, if you want. Or I don't have to. Whatever makes it easier."

"Stay? Please. We can just stay out here 'til everyone's gone. You can read me one of those books of yours or something."

"Okay. I can do that." He dug in his pocket, searching for the candy bars he'd brought, handing all three over.

"Thanks." Ardie opened one up and broke it in two, handing him half.

"You wanna go sit up in the loft? Up in our spot?" They had a place in the loft with a little cooler and blankets, a few books and magazines, a boom box.

Ardie nodded. "Yeah, okay." Ardie looked at him and managed a sad little smile. "I'm glad you came, West."

"You're my best friend, Ard. 'Course I'm here."

Ardie got up and grabbed his hand. "Let's make a run for it."

"'Kay." They started running and the distance to their safe little spot had never seemed so long.

They managed it without being seen, though, and flung themselves down onto the blankets, panting, Ardie still squeezing his hand.

"We can just stay here 'til everybody goes home." It was dim in here, cozy, quiet.

"Yeah," whispered Ardie. "Yeah."

They didn't say much, just sat, holding hands, shoulder to shoulder, watching the clouds outside the window.

"Thanks, West," whispered Ardie.

"Anything for you, yeah? Anything."

Anything.

"I feel the same way, West. Anything."

Ardie sniffed and they went back to being quiet. Waiting for the day to be over.

\*\*\*

The summer hadn't been too bad.

Everyone had said he was fourteen now, he could be the man of the house, he could take over the farm for his father. It was a good thing, too, because Momma'd kind of taken to her bed and not gotten up. But school'd started two weeks ago and now it was really hard. Really, really.

He was waiting on West to finish baseball practice and come see him and he was going to have to let West know. He couldn't do it. He couldn't do school and the chores and the crops and the critters. He just couldn't.

An ambulance pulled up, sirens wailing, right up to the school, Coach Benson carrying... West out. Oh, shit. Shit.

No. No, he couldn't do this again. He totally couldn't.

He ran up, pushing through the people starting to crowd around. "West! No!"

"Ardie! Go get Mom! My leg's hurt." West was all grey, but gave him a crooked smile. "I get to ride in an ambulance."

"You're going to be okay, West." He nodded and said it again. No way West was going to die on him. West wasn't allowed.

"I'm going to get a cast and entertaining drugs, Ard. Go. Get. My. Mom."

"'K, West." He took a last look at West, making sure his friend was really gonna be okay, and then he turned and ran as fast as he could to get Mrs. Moreland.

\*\*\*

Ardie sat in the waiting room, holding his hat, hating the smell, hating how this was just like with Poppa, waiting, waiting.

It had been the leg with Poppa, too, although there had been blood. So much blood.

And Poppa hadn't said anything, he'd never woken up after the thresher got his leg.

West was going to be all right. He *was*. He had to be.

"Ardie?" West's momma popped her head into the waiting room, dark hair all mussed. "You want to come sit with him while the cast sets?"

Ardie nodded. "I do, ma'am."

He got up and followed her, relief going through him. West was gonna be just fine if they were letting him in to sit with West.

West was sitting in one of the beds, looking a little goofy, a big old cast on his leg. "Ardie! Hey! It's broke in two places."

"Two? You don't do things by halves, do you?" He sat on the chair next to the bed, seeing West all right making him a little weak in his knees. "You look pretty happy for a guy with a broke-in-two-places leg."

West grinned. "They gave me a shot of something. Still... I hope you're wanting lots and lots of tutoring, Ard. I ain't playing baseball."

"Well, I'm sorry you're not playing baseball, West, but I sure could use your help with the studying. Well. I was on my way to tell you I was quitting school. I can't be there everyday, and do everything that needs doing around the farm, *and* homework. But if you were around to help with that more... Well, maybe I could stay in."

"You gotta stay in, Ardie. We'll make it all right, I promise."

"You think we can work it out with the teachers so I can skip classes? If you teach me in the evenings? It'll be all right once the snow comes, but 'til then? There's just too much to do, West." He hated unloading on West like this when his friend was all laid up in the hospital, but it had been eating at him since school started.

"I don't know. I'll talk to Mrs. Winters. It's illegal to quit, though. Two more years, you've got to go."

"Illegal to quit? But Ardie, I've got to run the farm. We can't lose it. We'd all get split up! Baby Luke's not even a year old yet, and the girls..." He blinked back his tears -- he was a big boy, dammit, and his Poppa was dead, and he had to step up and be the man. "We'll work it out. You always make the school stuff make sense, West."

"Ard. You gotta make your momma talk to the folks at the church. There's people to help."

"She won't leave the house. She won't talk. We can barely get her to get out of bed or to eat." He sighed and reached out, fingers rubbing on West's arm. "It'll ease up when the crops come in. Those church folks do help a lot, West. They're bringing food and helping with the laundry and stuff. But everyone's got crops to come in." It was a bad time to be asking for help. He didn't know if there was a good time to do it, but this wasn't it.

"I'll..." West took a deep breath. "I'll talk to my dad, too. He can help when he's not on the road."

"You don't have to do that, West." He knew that West didn't like asking favors of his father; never knew when his Dad was going to be in a good mood or was drunk.

"Yeah, I know, but I will." West gave him a smile, eyes rolling a little.

He grinned. "What about you? They going to let you go to school right away or do you get some time off to come and goof off at my place?"

"I get 'til Monday."

"Oh, man, you got gypped, that's not even a week. You shoulda broke it on Monday."

"Next time I'll remember." West winked at him, looking a little pale. "Did Mom say when I could go home?"

He shook his head. "No. Just that your cast had to dry. I'll stay with you 'til you go to sleep, 'kay?" Aggie and Mabel weren't expecting him back until the morning chores were needing to be done.

"Yeah? I'm not sleepy..." The words were broken up by a long yawn.

He laughed. "Sure you aren't, West. And my muscles don't ache at all."

"You work too hard." West frowned, sighed. "Too hard."

"Oh, I'll get used to it." He gave West a bright smile. "You don't need to worry 'bout me, West. You just try'n get better."

"I'm fine. Just a little cracked." He got a wink, West's eyes slow to open.

He laughed. "Sh. Billy Swaggert'll hear you and want you to supply him."

West chuckled, shook his head. "Billy's got bad breath. He's not allowed in the room."

That made him giggle. "You're crazy, West."

"Crazy like a fox, Ardie-Pardie."

"Anything you say, Westie-Testie."

"Westie-Testie? Testie?" West started giggling, the sound happy and familiar and dorky.

It made him feel good, that sound. Made him feel good he could make West laugh, too. "Well, you've got one or two, still, don't'cha?"

"Two, just like everybody else." West laughed harder.

"You sure? They've got you pretty drugged up and you never know what they had to take to save your leg." He tried to keep a straight face, but geez, a guy just couldn't.

"Eeew! I'd know! I'd know!"

He just rolled, was still wheezing from it when West's Momma came in, looking at them both like they'd lost their minds.

"They said you can get dressed, West. Ard, would you like to come over?"

"I gotta be home for chores before school tomorrow morning. I guess I'd best go home."

West's mom looked sad for a second. "Well, at least let me drive you home."

"That won't be too much on West?"

"I'll sit in the back seat, Ardie. It'll be cool."

West's mom nodded. "We'll stop and get McDonald's on the way."

He panicked a moment. No way he could afford McDonald's. "Oh, don't worry about me, I'm not hungry, and Aggie'n Mabel'll have done something up."

"It's our treat, Ardie. Honest. We'll get apple pies, too." West's mom gave him a warm smile. "Please."

"Yeah, Come on, Ard. Mmm... Big Macs."

"Okay." He smiled over at West. "I guess I could maybe stay for a bit. Long as I got home in time for chores in the morning."

"I promise. In time for bed, even." West's mom was pretty, when she was smiling.

"Thanks. I appreciate it."

He grinned at West and bounced a little even. It almost felt like a sleepover and they'd hardly gotten to spend anytime together since school started. Sure, West was hurt, but still...

"No problem. There's a phone in the lobby, if you want to call home."

He shook his head. "I called when they were working on West, told 'em I'd be home for chores tomorrow, but that was it."

"Excellent." West's mom's words trailed off when the nurse came in with a handful of pills and papers.

He ducked his head. "I'll get out of your way. Wait in the waiting room." He gave West a smile.

"See you in a minute, Ardie!"

He nodded and waved.

Sitting on the couch in the waiting room, he breathed a sigh of relief. West was okay. Everything else was just details.

\*\*\*

Christmas break? Rocked.

Well, it sort of sucked because of Ardie's dad, but still.

No school.

No school for two weeks.

That still rocked.

He and Ardie were putting lights up on the house, swaying on the rickety ladder.

"You be careful, West. Your Momma's gonna whip me good if I get your other leg broke."

He nodded, grinned over. He'd only had the cast off for a few weeks. The hurt leg was still littler than the other.

"Mrs. Wills said we shouldn't put up the decorations. That Poppa wasn't gone long enough. But the little ones deserve a nice time, don't they, West?"

"Your daddy wouldn't want y'all not to have a Christmas, Ardie. He liked Christmas."

Ardie nodded and smiled. "Yeah. He used to help Momma buy all our gifts." Ardie sighed and pulled out some more lights, carefully attaching them to the string they were putting up.

West didn't say anything. He and Mom had talked to the Baptist and the Methodist church ladies and there was a good Christmas coming.

"Sorry, West, I don't mean to be a wet blanket." Ardie gave him a smile. "I'll be more fun the rest of our break, I promise."

"You're cool, Ardie." He tacked another strand up.

Ardie nodded. "Cold even. Gonna maybe be a white Christmas this year." He got a wink.

"Wouldn't that be rocking cool? Snow?" Man, he'd love that. "Snowmen and sledding and snowball fights. It would be cool."

Ardie nodded and bounced slightly. "That would be rocking cool."

Oh, he was liking bouncing Ardie. For real.

Ardie was grinning up at him, watching him. "Don't fall," Ardie reminded him.

"I won't. Hand me another brad."

Ardie did, fingers sliding on his, chest against his legs.

Oh. He shook his head, lecturing himself a little. No thinking weirdo pervy thoughts about your best friend. You'd go to hell.

"You okay, West? You look a little funny."

"Yep. Just got something in my eye."

"'Kay." Ardie patted his leg and went back to sorting the strands of lights meant for the porch.

He started whistling -- Deck the Halls, with a little Santa Claus is Coming to Town in the middle. It felt good when Ardie started whistling along.

They got all the lights up and then headed back inside. "I think there's cobbler. Want some?"

"What kind?" He liked cherry, blueberry was nasty. "Is baby Luke talking yet?"

"Don't know, you'll have to ask Mabel. She likes you, though, so it's probably cherry, and yes." Ardie rolled his eyes. "Called me Bu-Pa."

"Bu-Pa? Where'd he come up with that?"

Ardie shrugged. "Aggie and Mabel call me Bubba, Patty calls me Poppa."

"It's cute." West grinned over, giggling. "Maybe I'll start calling you that, too."

"Oh, no, you don't!" Ardie shook his head. "I don't want 'em calling me Poppa, though, so I guess it'll do."

West looked down, sighed. "It ain't fair, Ardie. You deserve to have a real life."

"Life ain't fair, West. And I got a real life. This is it." Ardie bit his bottom lip, face earnest as he looked up. "I don't want to find a girl and settle with her anyway..."

"Well, you never have. Still, you work so hard." Like he was going to find a girl himself.

Ardie nodded. "I do work hard, but check this all out." Ardie turned and looked out over the farm. "This is mine, West. I work that earth, I feed those critters. I put food on the table." There was an awed pride in Ardie's voice.

"Yeah..." He smiled at Ardie, nodded. As soon as he could? He was out of this town. Going to college. Getting a real life. He wanted Ardie to come with him.

"So what did you get me for Christmas?" Ardie asked.

"A bundle of switches." He grinned over, shook his head. He had a neat set of speakers for the old truck Ardie was driving, a pair of fuzzy dice.

"No way! That's what I got you!" Ardie gave him a grin, bumped their hips together.

"We can put our bundles together, make a stack of switches."

Ardie laughed. "Your Momma gonna let you spend Christmas here?"

"She says I can come after church Christmas morning." He winked. "And stay 'til the second, if your mom's cool with it."

"No shit?" Ardie beamed at him. "That's awesome. Momma won't care."

"No shit. Mom's going on the truck with Daddy again." He hated spending the time alone. Luckily, Ardie's Momma was like a ghost, and never saw him really.

"Well, cool. I mean I'm sorry they're leaving you behind and all, but it's the best when you get to stay, West."

"Yeah, we'll watch the fireworks from the barn roof, yeah?"

"Sounds pretty damned good, West."

He nodded, pulled the ice cream from the freezer, and grabbed one of Ardie's school books from Patty.

Ardie got two pieces of cobbler out into bowls. "You're in luck. It's cherry cobbler."

"Yay!" West grabbed the spoons. "You want ice cream?"

"Does a bear shit in the woods?"

"Only if he doesn't live in the zoo or the polar icecap."

Ardie rolled his eyes. "Well, I don't live in the zoo or the polar icecap either, so I guess that must be a yes."

West laughed, scooped a big old scoop up and plopped it on the dessert. "You get through your midterms okay, Ardie?"

"I reckon I passed. Thanks to you." Ardie grabbed his bowl and sat at the big kitchen table. "Still not having enough time to finish the math questions."

"There'll never be enough time. So long as you get the ones you do right."

"I guess I'll find out when we go back into class. If I failed, though, I don't want to go back."

"You won't have failed. Ms. Carmichael's a nice lady." Everybody at the school was pulling for Ardie.

Ardie gave him a smile. "You always got faith in me."

"My job." He got his own ice cream. "You wanna watch a video?"

"Sure. Did you bring anything new? If not we can watch Terminator and Terminator 2 again. I like 'em."

"I got Indiana Jones and Ferris Bueller."

"Oh, that Harrison Ford is *dreamy*," said Aggie, coming in to bug them. "Ardie likes him, too."

"Shut up, Aggie."

"Well, you do. I saw you looking."

"Shut up." Ardie was looking at his cobbler like it was really really interesting.

"Harrison Ford is cool. I like his hat." West kept looking at Ardie, curious.

"Oh, I don't think it's his hat that Ardie likes."

"Agnes Carolyn Bodine, you go play with Mabel and leave me and West alone. Now."

Aggie stuck out her tongue and took off.

"Man, she's a pain in the ass." Ardie gave him a half smile.

"She's a sister. You keep telling me that's their job."

Ardie laughed, body easing a little, pink fading out of his cheeks.

"You okay, man? You look all wigged out." It happened more and more often, now that Ardie's dad was gone. West figured it was normal and shit, but still.

Weird.

"I'm good." Ardie nodded. "You done? Indiana Jones waits." Ardie's color got a bit high again and he ducked his head.

"Almost, yeah." He finished the last two bites and stood. "Movies, ho!"

Ardie laughed and joined him, the two of them sitting together on the couch.

"Which one you want to watch first?"

"I'm easy. They're all good."

"Well, I want to see Ferris Bueller's Day off," said Aggie, sitting next to West on the couch. "But Ardie's gonna want his date with Harrison Ford."

"Would you just go away, Aggie. *You* weren't invited."

"Don't be mean to your brother, Ag, or you'll get snakes from Santa."

"Yeah, and a big old lump of coal, too." Ardie leaned past him and smacked Agnes in the head. "Go *away*."

"Momma! Ardie hit me!"

Ardie rolled his eyes. "Just go, Agnes. You can watch Ferris when we're done with Indiana Jones, okay?"

"Fine." She stuck out her tongue again and flounced off.

"Girls." He settled back, rolled his eyes. "Least Luke's a boy."

"Yeah. Three sisters. Man, I'm cursed. I don't know why we need them anyway."

"Aggie's pretty cool, I guess." He shrugged. "Least she cooks a little."

Ardie snorted. "Mabel does most of it. Aggie's been a real pain since Poppa died. Like she's the only one whose life got affected.

"Is she... I mean, Mom says things get all weird when girls... You know, start." His cheeks were flaming. He knew how it worked, but *damn,* it sounded nasty.

Ardie made a face. "Ew, West. That's gross."

"I *know*! But maybe that's why she's bitchy."

Ardie shrugged. "I don't know, maybe." His friend shook his head. "I just don't get the big deal over girls. I mean that's gross stuff and it doesn't go away!"

"Don't ask me. I don't..." He shut his mouth. Fuck. Don't be *stupid*. Ardie was his very best friend.

Ardie gave him a look. "You think we're both just late bloomers, West?"

West looked down at the sofa. "I. I don't know."

"I meant what I said before, you know. I don't care if I don't have time to meet a girl, 'cause I don't want a wife."

"I don't either, Ard." He didn't, but he didn't want to say anymore. He didn't want to mess stuff up.

"Okay. Let's watch Harrison Ford."

"Okay. Wanna turn the light off so there's no glare?"

"Sure."

Ardie got up and turned off the light and when he came back they were sitting shoulder to shoulder.

Aggie was right. Harrison Ford was hot. Really.

\*\*\*

Ardie couldn't believe it was New Year's Eve already. The week with West had flown by, full of fun and laughter. They hadn't had this much free time together since before Poppa died and he enjoyed every moment of it.

Even Aggie's teasing, Mabel's big, quiet eyes, Momma's non-appearance; none of those could ruin it for him.

He and West had helped get Tricia and Luke suppered and settled. Aggie was headed off to some party, and Mabel was watching TV in Momma's room. He and West had the rest of the evening to themselves.

It'd warmed up a little, so they grabbed some blankets and pillows, sodas and chips, the flashlight, and West's ever present books and headed up to the roof.

It didn't take anytime at all before they'd made themselves a nest and were cuddled together under one of the blankets -- because it turned out it wasn't *that* warm -- looking at the stars in the sky. West knew what all the constellations were and could tell the stories of each one. Ardie just listened, fascinated, even when he'd heard the story before.

West's voice had finally broken this fall and it was deeper than it used to be, not as deep as Ardie's was, but deep enough that West sounded like a man now instead of a boy. Ardie liked that, liked listening to West rumble on.

The fireworks started up when the sky got good and dark -- all reds and purples and bright. "Man, I wish I was a firework. All bright and shit," West said.

"Yeah, but once you've exploded, bam -- you're done."

"Yeah... I think that's still kind of cool, don't you?"

"I don't know. I'd kind of miss you if you got all used up quick." He cuddled a little closer, shivering. He didn't want to lose West like he'd lost his Dad.

"You ever thought about what you're gonna do after high school?"

"What is there to think about? I'll work the farm." He hadn't even considered anything else after Poppa'd passed.

"Well... Nothing, I guess." West looked out at the fireworks, shrugged. "Just asking."

He looked over at West, at his friend's face as the colors from the fireworks lit it up. "What about you? You could work it with me, you know. I could use the help."

"Me?" He got a shocked, vaguely wigged out look. "Ardie, I'm getting the hell out of here. I'm set up to take my SATs in the spring, then start applying to colleges."

"Oh." Oh, he hadn't even thought. He'd figured. Oh. "You're in a hurry to go, huh?" Oh, man, he'd never expected that. He'd thought they were gonna be friends forever.

"In a hurry? I don't guess so. I just... There's so much world out there, Ardie. So much we ain't seen. 'Sides you, there's no reason to stay."

"Oh." And he guessed he wasn't reason enough. Funny how that kind of hurt, but not as much as the thought of West going. God, that... he'd always taken it for granted that him and West were gonna be best friends forever.

He maybe even had been hoping recently that just maybe, seeing as West never seemed to look at girls like *that* either, that just maybe him and West would be more than just friends.

Think again, Ardie.

West looked over at him, sighed. "We'll be friends forever, Ard. I swear it. I just gotta go to college, go to school and stuff. It's important."

He nodded. "Yeah. I just didn't think about it, really." He gave West a smile. "I guess I figured you'd find something to do around here. It was silly."

"Well, I guess you love this farm. I got an old bed and a shit-load of books. It's different." West shrugged. "Beside, Mom and Daddy are selling the house when I go."

"Sell the house? But where will you stay when you come back for holidays and summers and stuff?"

"What? You're not gonna invite me?"

"Since when do you need an invitation?"

"Well, then. I'm coming to stay with you. Dork."

"Well, okay, then. You'd better, too." He nudged West and went back to watching the fireworks, feeling a little better about things.

"I think we should spend every New Year's Eve like this." West grinned. "Forever."

That made him happy, all the way through. He nodded. "Yeah, I could handle that."

"Cool." West leaned back, watching. "I like the purple ones best."

"I like the ones that fill the whole sky."

"There'll be lots of those at midnight. You know it's already tomorrow in England?"

"No shit? They missed the fireworks then." West knew all kinds of stuff like that. West was the smartest person he knew. Smarter even than the teachers he bet.

"I bet they just did them earlier and shit. I want to visit there one day. There and Japan."

"Japan? Wow. That's really foreign." West had the neatest dreams. "Long as you always come back," he murmured quietly.

"Well, yeah. Maybe you'll come with me sometimes." West looked over, eyes grinning behind those horn-rimmed glasses.

"I don't know. Maybe." It could be nice, traveling with West. Maybe away from here they could talk about the feelings he was having for West. Maybe West would understand, because he wasn't like most of the people here. He was smarter and better.

"It would be cool. We could go to Egypt, climb on pyramids."

"Ride camels?" He could dream right on next to West. Hell, once Luke was old enough to be on his own, he'd have a lot more free time in the winter.

"Oh, yeah! Look for mummies and stuff. It'll be too cool."

"What about Australia? I always thought that was neat, them being on the other side of the world like that."

"Oooh... boomerangs are wicked cool. And kangaroos. And they sound too cool when they talk."

"I know you're smarter than me, West, but I think you're wrong about kangaroos talking..."

West's laughter could just fill the whole sky. He watched his friend's face all lit up with it, watched as another firework exploded, shadowing West's face in red.

Oh. West was... handsome.

"Man, Ardie -- You're a funny guy. Maybe you should become a stand-up comedian. You could be the next Robin Williams or something."

Oh, that made *him* laugh so hard he snorted. "Nobody but you thinks I'm funny, West. 'Sides, I don't like going up on stage and talking in front of all those people. Bad enough when I've got to do the reading at church."

He was still smiling, though, almost beaming. West sure made him feel good. Special. Almost as special as West was... He sat up suddenly. Oh, lord. He had it bad. Real bad. For his best friend.

"Ard? Ard, you okay? Something bite you?"

He blinked, looking over at West, feeling himself start getting hard. Oh, man. Oh, God, what was he gonna do? "I'm fine. Thought I heard Tricia calling. I should go check."

"Okay. You want me to come with?" West gave him a lopsided grin, pushed his glasses up.

"Naw, it's probably nothing. No need for us both to go."

He managed a smile back and fled, nearly falling off the roof in his eagerness to get out of sight and give his prick a strong talking to. No getting hard over his best friend. God, West would go and never come back.

He went and checked on Tricia and Luke, deflating as he went. Thank God. Then he went and got them a couple more sodas, putting an ice cube down his pants. That would keep him from popping up again.

"Weren't nothing," he told West when he got back onto the roof. "So I brought us some more sodas."

Damn, West still looked amazing. Good thing there was still a bit of ice not melted yet.

"Cool. You didn't miss nothin' here."

Sure he had; he'd missed five whole minutes of time with West. Which he was starting to see might just be pretty special. But he just smiled and settled back under the blanket, trying really hard not to get too close and rub himself all over West. Like he kind of wanted to.

"So, you making any resolutions? I don't know if I am or not." West rambled on, drinking his Coke and watching the fireworks.

Ardie lay on his belly, watching West as much as the sky. "I'd like to do better at school, but I'm already trying as hard as I can, so I'm not sure a resolution would make any difference."

"You're doing it. You'll graduate. You just keep doing what you're doing."

"Well, then, you'd better keep doing what you're doing, 'cause I'm only making it through thanks to you." He nudged West's hip with his own. "You've been a real life-saver, West."

"That's what friends do. You help me when I need it."

He nodded. He just seemed to need it more. But as long as West was happy, so was he. "What about you? Any resolutions?"

"I don't think so. Try to stay out of trouble, maybe?" West shrugged. "I just don't have much to change. Maybe get a car."

No, West was pretty good just the way he was. "You know I don't mind driving you 'round, right?"

"Yeah, I know. And we have fun, don't we?"

"Hell, yeah. And this summer? We can do drive-ins. It'll be a blast."

"Oooh, yeah. There's still one out there near Bowls. That would be cool."

"Yeah, would be like a da-" He shut his stupid mouth quick. "Damn good," he finished up, but it was pretty weak.

West looked at him a little, then nodded. "Yeah. Damn good."

He grinned and nodded and rested his head on his hands. "Wanna read me the next chapter of that robot book?"

"Sure." West opened the book. "Where were we?"

"They just figured out the robots were doing stuff they hadn't been programmed to do."

"Cool." West started reading, voice filling the air, punctuated by the fireworks.

He watched West's face change colors with every new round of fireworks, listened to his friend's voice. And if his interest wasn't entirely innocent? Well, he wasn't going to tell anyone, and he imagined neither was the roof.

\*\*\*

Man, it had been a quick, quick summer.

West had a sweet little job at the lake in the sno-cone truck. Had some cash. Had a tan. Had a jock boyfriend from UT who was showing him things he never even knew to look for.

Shit.

Still, he'd not seen near enough of Ardie, and had told David he had family stuff he had to do on his day off this week, and drove out to the farm, bouncing and eager to spend some time.

He pulled up, finding Mabel and Tricia on the front porch, shelling peas.

"Hi, West, long time no see. Ardie's out back under the tractor." She smiled ruefully. "Just follow the swearing."

"Cool." He grabbed the bag of Cokes and chips he'd brought, heading around back. "Hello? You back here, Ardie-Pardie?"

There was a bang and a clang and a quiet 'fuck' and then Ardie pushed himself out from under the old tractor. "West? Hey! Good to see you."

"Hey, stranger." He held out a Coke. "Thirsty."

"Hell, yeah."

Ardie stood and wiped his hands off on his pants before giving West a big hug. "Man, it feels like forever." Ardie's eyes were on him, just drinking him in.

"I know it! It's hell being a working man." He grinned, leaned into Ardie a little. "How's things here?"

"Pretty good on the farm front. Not so great on the Agnes front. She's making life hell and Momma doesn't give a shit. I don't know why I should, except there is no one else." Ardie sighed and kind of leaned back. "Man, it's good to see you. Wanna go to the loft? Or out to the creek?"

"Whichever, man. I'm yours 'til Thursday afternoon."

Adie beamed at him. "Excellent. Come on, let's go up to the loft. Our hidey-hole's still up there and I don't want to be found."

"Cool." He nodded, walking with Ard, heading toward the old barn. "Man, it seems like this summer is just motoring along. I've scooped up more sno-cones than you can imagine."

"I'll bet. I can't believe this," murmured Ardie, grabbing his arm and testing his muscles. "Just look at you."

"Man, those scooper muscles? Massive." They looked at each other, started laughing.

"God, I've missed you, West." Ardie gave him a one-armed hug and then started up the ladder into the loft.

"I hear you. I never thought things would get so busy so fast." Especially having a guy to... play with. Made it hard to just leave and visit.

Ardie nodded and settled into their nest. "I miss you," he said softly.

"I miss you, too, man. I can't wait for school to start, things to be normal again. David's leaving for Austin, soon. The job'll be over."

Ardie gave him a look. "Who's David?"

"A guy I'm s... I met at the lake. He's a shortstop for UT. Nice guy." Great kisser.

"You're hanging out with college guys?"

"He hung out with me, really. I'm sort of in the sno-cone box." West grinned, blushed, not sure how much he could say.

Ardie frowned. "Why would a college guy want to hang around your sno-cone box?"

"Maybe because he thinks I'm fine, Ardie." The words sort of popped out, fueled by pride, by a little anger. He wasn't as buff as Ardie, but he wasn't butt-ugly.

Ardie sat up and he could see Ardie put it together. "And you let a guy that thought you were fine hang out with you? You hung out at more than just the sno-cone box, didn't you."

"Well... I mean, yeah. Sometimes. Late after work."

"So... " Ardie looked down at his hands. "Is this why you don't date girls?"

"I... Are you gonna be pissed at me if I say yes, Ard?" Because he'd lie, if Ard wouldn't be mad.

Ardie looked back up at him, looked right in his eyes. "No."

"Okay. 'Cause... I'm not gonna date girls. Ever."

"So you and this UT shortstop. You? You know?"

"Yeah. Sort of. I mean. Yeah." His cheeks were burning, eyes on Ard's shoe.

"Wow." He wasn't sure if Ard was sounding awed or grossed out.

"Yeah." He didn't know what to say, so he just nodded.

"Yeah." Ardie nodded, too, and looked at him again, something unreadable flitting across his face. "So I guess that's why you haven't been coming by that much."

"Well, not just that. I am working a lot. I see Dave after. Honest."

"Yeah?" Ardie bit his lip, played with his Coke can. "So I guess you're not such a slow bloomer after all."

"I guess. I haven't. I mean, we don't... It's not like heavy stuff, Ard." God, this was embarrassing.

Ardie snorted. "I've never even kissed anyone, West. So I'd say you're blooming faster'n me."

"Well, it's pretty cool. I mean, what I've done of it's pretty cool."

"He treating you right?" Ardie asked, voice rough, a little bit fierce.

"I guess?" West sighed, opened the chips. "I don't know. I've never done this before, Ardie. I mean, do I ask for his number in Austin? Do I tell him where I live? I don't know."

"Well, if he's just using you, you'd best know that now, and I'll go beat his ass to a pulp," growled Ardie.

He grinned over, took a swig of his soda. "It's weird -- I mean, I've thought maybe I was, you know, for a while, but I never knew for sure."

"What made you decide for sure?"

"Dave, I guess. He kept coming by and saying stuff and I... I mean, I don't know about being in love or anything, but I'm in something. Probably trouble."

"You know I meant what I said about kicking his ass, right, West? I'm your best friend and any trouble finds you, finds me." It had always been like that, since that first day of school when Henry Martin had picked on him.

He could always count on Ardie to have his back and it looked like that hadn't changed because he was gay.

"Thanks, Ard." He smiled over, feeling more settled than he had in weeks. "Man, I've missed the hell out of you."

Ardie grinned at him, nodded. "I never thought I'd be saying I can't wait for school to start again, but it sure will be nice to see more of you, even if it is for studying."

"Yeah. Well, I may just tell Dave he'll have to not hang with me on my days off 'cause I'm busy, yeah?" Unless Ardie wanted to meet Dave.

"You'd do that?" Ardie beamed at him. "I sure would like to see you more than once a month, West."

"Well, sure, Ard. He's a guy. You're... Ardie."

Ardie just grinned at him. "Quit hogging the chips, Westie-Testie."

"Bitch." He handed over the bag, laughing hard.

"Oh, no, I'm all stud." Ardie was laughing, too, snickering and grinning just like old times.

West just hooted, laughing so hard his belly hurt. "Man, you're a funny guy, Ard."

Ardie nodded. "I ought to charge you per laugh."

"What? I only make $4 an hour. I'd be broke."

Ardie chuckled. "But you're the only one who thinks I'm funny, so if I'm gonna make it as a comedian, you need to start paying me."

"You just don't use your best stuff with anyone else, Ard."

Ardie shrugged and smiled for him. "So you're liking the sno-cone business?"

"I like the money. I like people watching. I hate the way my hands get all sticky."

"And you like the company," teased Ardie, foot nudging his leg.

"Well, yeah." His cheeks turned bright red, but he nodded. "And the view."

Ardie laughed, but not meanly.

"Y'all ought to all come. I'd give everybody a freebie."

"Yeah? Maybe we will. Stuff everyone in the truck and drive up for a picnic. Would you be able to eat with us?"

"Sure, if you came up around eleven. My shift starts at noon."

Ardie nodded. "I'll talk to the girls. They'd like to get out to the water, I bet. Mabel makes a mean fried chicken now."

"Really? Wow. How... What about your mom? Is she getting any better?" He found himself hating Ardie's mom sometimes, for falling apart and not taking care of her kids and making Ardie do it.

Ardie's face closed up and he shook his head. "Mabel sometimes gets her to talk, but mostly she lies in bed and watches TV. Though, I think she'd be just as happy lying there not watching anything. It's only on, 'cause Mabel turns it on." Ardie bit his lip and then looked up at West. "You know anything about girls?"

"Like what?"

Ardie sighed. "Agnes... she's been real... well, testy and it ain't just at her time, it's all the time, and I just don't know what to do about her. She's hanging out with Henry Martin's younger brother and with a bunch of other boys who are older'n her and I think she's, you know doing it."

West's eyes went wide. "But she's a *baby*, Ardie."

They were both sixteen now, but Aggie wasn't even near that old.

"I *know*, West. I tried talking to her. I tried threatening her. I tried getting Momma to talk to her." Ardie shook his head. "She hates me, and I think I'm making it worse."

"You want me to talk to my mom about it? Or maybe you could talk to the counselor at school?"

"Could you, West? I don't... I'll talk to Mr. Jonas in September if things don't get better, but I'd sooner not involve anyone official if I don't have to. Poppa'd want me to make sure the family stays together, West. And I'm trying my best, I really am."

"I'll talk to Mom. She'll know what to do. She's smart that way." He reached out, squeezed Ard's hand. "You're the best, Ard. For real."

"No. You are." Ardie squeezed back and gave him a warm smile.

"Shit. I just do good at school stuff. You're like raising a whole family."

"And you're my best friend. You're good to me. Better'n anyone I know."

"My job." He winked. "Ardie-Pardie."

"Well, you're good at it." Ardie paused. "Testie-Westie."

They laughed together, long and loud. Yeah, yeah. He'd needed this.

Needed Ard.

\*\*\*

Ardie was glad when school started again. Despite the fact that he was way busier, he got to see more of West, and he knew West wasn't seeing that David fella every day anymore.

It wasn't that Ardie didn't like David. He'd met the guy two times when he and the kids had gone to see West at his sno-cone job and he'd tried real hard to not like David. But David was nice and seemed to treat West nice.

The problem was that Ardie wanted to be the one with West. Only he'd lost his chance, hadn't he? If he'd been brave like West, and told West that he liked guys and not girls, maybe West would be with him instead of someone else.

He sighed, peeking at West from under his lashes as they sat together at the big kitchen table working on their studying. West sure was growing up handsome.

West had bought himself contacts with his summer money, got his hair cut, too. Suddenly it was like West's eyes were huge and really green and bright.

Ardie knew he'd pretty much do anything West asked, but those eyes? They sealed the deal.

And they gave him thoughts. Like how they'd look up really close if he were to try kissing West, and how they'd look if he told West he liked guys, too, and... He sighed again and looked back at his books. West already had a boyfriend. And even if he didn't, West had big plans to see the world and he had the farm and a family to take care of.

"What's wrong, Ard? You know how to do those equations. You rocked at them last year."

"What? Oh. I'm just tired is all." He managed to find a smile for West. God, he had to get with it.

"You need some help with your chores? I will, you know." West smiled back, eyes warm.

"I know. You could stay the weekend. With your help the chores and my homework wouldn't take too long. We could do stuff after." Like a date, only not, because him and West were just friends.

"Sure. I was sorta hoping Dave could call, say he could come visit, but he hasn't." West shrugged. "I bet college is busy."

Oh, wow. Yeah, of course West wanted to be with Dave on a Saturday night. It was what you did; you saw your sweetheart, even if it was another guy. "You could call him, if you'd rather."

"No... He... He doesn't want me to call." West turned pink, looked away. "Anyway, we'll have fun. Terrorize the girls."

"Wait a second, West. He doesn't want you to call? Why not?" West deserved the best. The absolute best.

"Well, if you were in college, would you want your buddies to know you were dating a kid?"

"If it was you? I'd tell them to go to hell."

"Yeah, but you're my best friend, Ard. Nobody sticks up for me like you do."

"Well, the guy you're dating should," he muttered.

"Yeah, well, I'm starting to maybe think he wasn't dating, just me."

"You mean he was using you? You got his number? Know where he lives? I'll go kick his ass for you, West, 'cause that ain't right." He'd kick that Dave's ass so hard his nuts would come out his throat.

West reached out, grabbed his hand. "Might as well kick mine for thinking it might be something besides a few kisses and some necking at the lake."

He turned his hand to hold onto West's. "He was there every day, West, what were you supposed to think?" Then he squeezed West's hand. "I'm sorry."

"Yeah. Well, it just means my time's more free for school and hanging out, right?"

He grinned, hand sliding away before he started to read more into it than he should. "Yeah. So we're good for this weekend? You need to call your momma and let her know?"

"I'll go home and grab some clothes and a couple movies, if you want."

"That'd be cool." He smiled over at West, glad this David was idiot enough not to hold onto West. Not that he wanted West to be unhappy, but he was glad to have West around again.

"Cool. I got some chips and stuff, too. I'll bring 'em. You wanna come with?"

"Yeah. I wanna check out your ride." He grinned. West had a brand-new used car. Too cool.

"It's pretty cool. Has a kick-ass stereo system." West almost bounced, leading him out to the bronze Oldsmobile.

"And she runs, right?" He grinned. "That's always a selling point." He went over to the front of the car. "Let's see what she's got under the hood."

West popped the hood, exposing a nice little 6-cylinder, clean as a whistle.

"Oh, this is nice, West." He nodded, checking things out carefully. "This is real nice."

"Thanks. Dad's friend Elmer sold it to me. I paid for half and my folks got the other half."

"That's cool. A lot nicer looking than a beat up old truck, too." He grinned at West, nudged their hips together. "Come on, let's go open her up on the road."

"You got it." West hopped in and started her up, the radio blaring.

Chuckling, he got into the passenger seat and rolled down his window. It was still more than warm enough for them to go cruising with the windows open.

He was glad he wasn't stupid like Dave; he knew he had a good thing in West. The best.

# Chapter Three

He headed over to the farm, a bunch of kitchen stuff from the house in his car. Mom and Dad had sold the house quicker than anyone had expected, both of them going to live on the road, and he was giving Ard and them all the extras.

He wasn't going to need them at the dorms.

There wasn't much left -- a couple more loads here and there, but basically, it was done. He wasn't sure if it was exciting or sad.

Ardie was on the porch, arguing with Agnes, who screamed as he pulled up and went running off. Ardie sighed, and managed a smile for him. "Hey, West."

"Hey, Ard. What's up?" He started pulling out stuff to carry in.

Ardie shook his head. "Just the usual. Thanks for all this. It'll help." Ardie grabbed some stuff and headed inside with it.

West followed, nodded to little Luke as they passed. "Hey, Luke. There's a box of Matchbox cars in the trunk, all for you."

"Bu-Pa! Didja hear?"

"I did, Luke; go on see if you can find it."

"It's the blue plastic box, 'kay? It's a little heavy." He chuckled, shook his head. "That boy thinks you hung the moon."

"It makes kind of a nice change to Aggie," Ardie said wryly.

"She *still* getting in trouble? She's something else, Ard." Something else and kind of a slut, too, though he'd never say it.

"Well, it depends on how you look at it. I think she's in trouble, she says she's not." Ardie shot him a look. "We're going to need diapers again around here in a bit."

He stopped still, blinked. "You don't mean..."

"She's gonna have a baby. And she won't tell me who the father is, says he's not interested in it, so that's that." Ardie shook his head. "He should be standing by her, he should. You would if it had been you; me, too. But these kids she's hanging out with..." Ardie sighed. "Luke's in school next year, and by then there'll be another one in diapers..."

"Christ. Christ, Ard." He looked over, took a deep breath. "Can't she give it up or get an abortion? Can't your mom make her?"

"Momma hasn't been out of bed in months," Ardie said quietly. "And Aggie said she's keeping it. I don't see how I can fight her -- I'm not her legal guardian."

"Then let's get the papers drawn up so you are." That familiar dislike of Ardie's mother rose up again. "What if Luke gets sick, Ard?

Make that woman sign everything over. If you have to give up your whole damn life, you ought to have control over it!"

"I'm worried if we involve the law they're going to just see her lying in bed all day and take the young ones away."

"You're grown now, Ard. It's not the police; it's a lawyer thing. You *have* to."

Ardie bit his lower lip and then nodded. "Yeah. I guess I should. If something happened to Luke and she couldn't sign and he got hurt I'd never forgive myself."

West nodded, thanking God he'd thought enough to give Ardie a good reason. Fact was, it wasn't fair for Ardie to work so hard for nothing.

"Will you go with me, West? I'll make an appointment with Poppa's lawyer tomorrow. If you come, you can explain the bits I'm not sure on."

"Sure. Sure, I will." He found Ard a smile. "Always." Well, until he left for college in August...

"Thanks." Ardie ran his hand over his short hair and sighed. "I don't know what I'm going to do when you're gone."

"Call a lot." West bumped hips with him, grinned. "A whole lot."

Ardie laughed. "Yeah. Yeah, you're gonna cost me a bundle in long distance, I can tell." Ardie headed back toward the car. "Let's get the rest of this shit unloaded so we can go fishing."

"Sounds good. Hey, I'm going to bring all my books over and the bookshelves. Will you keep them for me?"

"Anything you want, West." Ardie leaned over the car, pulled out some more stuff and hoisted it, muscles bulging under his T-shirt.

West let himself admire for a second, then dug out the box for Luke, putting it up on the porch.

They soon had it all unpacked and Ardie gave him a grin. "Ice cream?"

"Oh, yeah. There Coke in the fridge?" He went to wash his hands -- man, he was filthy.

"Yeah, you want floats?" Ardie joined him at the sink, pushing and shoving with him for the water.

He splashed a little. "Nah. I just want both. Greedy me."

"You don't get what you don't ask for, right?"

Ardie splashed more than a little chortling when he managed a particularly good aim and got West full on. West grabbed the sprayer, turning it on Ardie, catching him good, the cold water making the white T-shirt see through. Ardie laughed, trying to wrestle the sprayer from his hands, muscles just working. Damn, working on the farm had left Ardie *built*.

"Don't you two get my floor wet!" Mabel sounded peeved, glaring across the kitchen.

Ardie chuckled and winked at him, eyes aiming back toward his sister. He nodded and they turned together, soaking Mabel to the skin, laughing at her squeal.

Still chuckling, Ardie turned off the water. "Tell Aggie I said she had to mop up the mess, and if she has a problem with it, she comes to see me. You want some ice cream, Mabel?"

"Yeah; gimme some to take up to Momma, too, you hooligan."

Ardie laughed at her, and West thought that if Ardie had to grow up fast, Mabel had to grow up like lightning.

West shook his head, grinned. "You gonna come see me in college, Mabel? Find you a college man?"

Mabel snorted. "Tell you what -- you find someone who'll take Aggie and beat some sense into her, and I'll be more'n happy with that."

Ardie rolled his eyes. "Always practical, our Mabel."

"Someone's got to be."

Ardie nodded. "Yeah. Yeah, they do."

West nodded. "I'm sorry, Mabel. My mom tried to help. Aggie's just..."

Aggie.

"A selfish little bitch."

"Mabel!" Ardie sounded shocked.

"Well, it's *true*, Maynard Bodine, and you know it."

Ardie sighed. "You shouldn't use language like that, though, Mabel."

Mabel rolled her eyes. "I'm not a little girl anymore, Ardie, just like you're not a boy no more."

West nodded, not sure what to say. The whole thing was so unfair, so wrong. Ardie should be going to college, too. Mabel should be looking for boyfriends.

Ardie dished up two bowls of ice cream and put them on a tray for Mabel, giving her a kiss on her cheek. She gave her older brother a smile. "Thanks, Bu-Pa." Ardie growled at her, but there was no heat in it.

"You want vanilla or chocolate, West?"

"Vanilla." He grabbed a towel and wiped up the water before somebody fell and broke something.

Ardie soon had them set up with bowls of ice cream and glasses of Coke. "You're going to miss all this when you go, West. I mean, wiping up floors? You don't find that kind of glamour in the city."

"Oh, I'll have mad crazy parties where I'll be the youngest and wiping beer off the floors, I'm sure." He winked over, grinned. "Besides, I'll be around for Thanksgiving, yeah? Then Christmas, if you'll have me?"

"You don't come back for Christmas and I'll come up there and bring you back myself."

West grinned, warm all through. "It's a deal."

"I still can't believe we're graduated. Or that you're really going."

"I'm real proud that you did it, Ard. Lots of folks would've quit."

Ardie snorted. "Like you'd let me quit."

"Nope. You deserved to graduate. It's important."

"Yep. I can't kick Luke and Tricia's asses about it if I didn't."

West nodded. "What about Aggie? Is she gonna stay in?"

Ardie shook his head. "Shit, West, your guess is as good as mine."

"Yeah." He sighed, nodded. "Well, just remember it's her baby, not yours. Don't let her dump everything on you."

"I won't kick her out, West. Or her baby. That's my niece or nephew she's got in her belly."

"I didn't say kick her out. I said..." He sighed, shook his head. "Never mind. Nothing I say'll matter."

"That's not true, West and you know it."

"I just worry about you. I don't want you to be taken advantage of."

Ardie smiled at him. "Gotta look after my family, West. I consider you a part of that, yeah?"

"Yeah. Yeah, I know, Ard. It's one of the coolest things about you."

Ardie chuckled. "You *need* to go to the city if you think *I*'m cool."

West snorted. "Freak. I said it was one of the coolest things *about* you."

"Oh, so now I'm uncool, am I?" Ardie's eyes were twinkling at him.

"Maybe just a little..." He moved away from Ard's hands, sliding out of Ard's reach.

"Yeah, I see you moving, Westie-Testie."

"That's *Mr.* Westie-Testie to you."

Ardie laughed and leaned over, smacking his ass.

"Oooh!" They started laughing harder, both of them teasing and shoving, joking.

It was great, seeing Ardie laugh, relax and be a teenager instead of the serious man he'd grown into.

West was going to miss him, so fucking much.

*** 

Ardie was excited.

West had missed coming home for Thanksgiving and Christmas. It had probably been for the best; Aggie'd been a royal bitch and they'd all been short with each other and definitely lacking the holiday spirit.

But it was May now and more than time for West to come home.

The last eight months he'd missed West hard.

And he thought he was going to take his shot. Tell West he was gay, too. And tell West there was only one man he was interested in.

Luke was on car duty, watching for Uncle West's bronze Olds.

Ardie was pretending he wasn't sitting on the porch watching for it, too. Every now and then he'd snore a little, making Luke giggle.

It wasn't an Oldsmobile that pulled up, though. It was a little bright red Honda, West behind the wheel, longish hair flying.

He got up and headed out to the path, shaking his head. "Look at what the cat dragged in." He could feel the grin tugging at his lips, something hard inside him easing.

"Ard!" West tumbled out, skinnier than ever, sunglasses perched on his nose. "God, it's been forever."

"Eight months of forever." He went right up to West and wrapped him in a bear hug.

West surprised him by pressing close, holding on for a long time. "It's good to see you."

"Yeah, you, too, West." He held on a moment longer, squeezed and then gave West a look. "You okay, buddy?"

"Just been a long couple months." West grabbed a knapsack, gave him a smile.

"You should have come home at Christmas." He put his arm around West's shoulders and steered West in, headed for the guest room.

"Yeah. I should have." West put his bag down, sat on the bed. "I'm here 'til mid-July at least, maybe late August, if I get a job."

"You wanna talk about it?" he asked, sitting next to his best friend. He hated seeing West look so... defeated.

"Oh, it's nothing. Same old crap. Too much homework, too many parties, too many guys. Too much competition for the right guys."

"Oh, I'll bet you're one of the right guys." Ardie was rethinking telling West how he felt. It might be kind of silly, him thinking West might be interested in him like that when there were a whole bunch of college boys from all over to choose from. With the farm and his sisters, Luke and Aggie's new baby, he wasn't the world's best catch.

West grinned. "No. No, I'm not. But thanks, Ard."

He snorted. "I thought those college boys were supposed to be smart?"

"They are. Smart enough to make a fool out of me. You going to let me meet the new baby?"

"You know it. She's a pretty little girl. Already got us all wrapped around her fingers." Just like her Momma. Agnes was already back to her old ways, leaving the baby with him and Mabel, and he was having a hard time finding it in him to care -- little Alice was a sweetheart.

"Cool. How's Mabel doing? Still managing school?" West stood, let him lead them into the front room.

"Yeah. She's got a head on her shoulders and Aggie was good enough up until about a month ago. Weather got warmer and she got itchy feet again." He shrugged. "She's just lost and I don't know how to help her." He'd been mad at her for awhile, frustrated that she wouldn't grow up, but he'd come to think that one of them should have a time to rebel, be a kid.

"Have you considered a good, hard beating?"

He laughed. "Damn, I've missed you, West."

He stopped and gave West another tight hug and then opened the door into Aggie's room, the baby in her crib, having a nap.

"I'm not surprised she's still napping -- she was up half the night. Poor thing's a little croupy."

"What the fuck does that mean?" West whispered, peering in. "She's little."

"I don't know, something with her stomach and gas. All I know is it means she screams unless you walk her up and down and sometimes even then. Poor thing." He smiled down at the wee baby. "Just you wait until she's awake. She has the most amazing green eyes."

"Yeah? Cool. Did you get the stuff I sent? I thought she'd be cute dressed up as a university cheerleader?"

He chuckled. "She will be. Once she grows into them. I don't know who her daddy was, but he has to have been small, 'cause Aggie's big-boned like me, but she's just little and delicate."

As if she knew they were talking about her, little Alice woke up, mouth opening before eyes, just like always. Chuckling, Ardie reached in and picked her up, cradling her. "You wanna hold her, West?"

West's eyes got wide and he backed up, shook his head. "No. That's cool. You're good."

He grinned; he'd been pretty nervous the first few times, too. "It's not that much different from holding a calf or pig or kitten. You sure you don't want to?"

"I'm pretty sure. If I dropped her, you'd kill me."

He chortled. "Lord love a duck -- you wouldn't drop her, West."

He took Alice over to the changing table and took care of her diaper like the expert he was. Luke had been good practice for Alice. She was cuter, though, something about the way those big eyes always found him, the way that little hand wrapped around his finger...

"Man, you're going to be a great dad."

"Nope. I already am a great uncle. That's gonna have to do me." He gave West a smile.

West grinned. "Yeah. I'll just be a marginal best friend of the great uncle."

"Never marginal, West. You've got pride of place at my table, anytime you want it."

"Thanks, man." West walked up behind him, leaned in close and looked over his shoulder. "She's cute."

"Yeah. She is." He grinned down at Alice, finger finding her ribs, making her kick and giggle and for just a moment, it was perfect, West's heat leaning against him, little Alice laughing up at them.

"Oh, she's pretty." West's cheek moved against his arm in a grin.

He nodded and picked her up, holding her so she and West could get a good look at each other. "This is your Uncle West, Alice. Yes, he is. You say hi really nice now."

She looked good and hard, then reached out and grabbed West's hair and pulled. Hard.

"Oh! Sorry, West." He was trying hard not to laugh, trying to undo that amazingly strong baby-grip.

"Is this is the Bodine family way of telling me I need a hair-cut?"

He did laugh then, snuggling Alice against him, worried he was gonna drop her. "Well, it is a little long, Westonbury Moreland."

"I'm going to get it cut. It's on the list."

"I've got a pair of clippers. We could do it for you." He gave West a wink, enjoying the closeness. He'd missed this the last eight months. Missed his best friend like crazy.

West's eyes went wide again, playful. "Oh, I don't think so. I want a cut, not to be piebald."

He laughed. "Damn. We were gonna send Aggie out to be a barber -- how's she supposed to practice?"

"She's got you and Luke..." West winked over, grinning wide.

"Yellow belly," he accused, holding up Alice as protection.

"My belly is not!" West lifted his shirt, exposing a flat belly and the hint of a dark something creeping around the small of his back.

"Whoa. What the hell?" Had someone hit West? "What's this?" he asked, one hand keeping West from putting his shirt back down.

"Nothing, man. A mistake." West backed up, pulling his shirt down.

"Somebody hit you?" he growled, whole body going tight.

Alice started crying and Ardie strode out into the hall, finding Tricia and plopping the baby in her arms. "Find Aggie, tell her to take care of her daughter."

"Chill out, Ard."

He turned around, hands on his hips. "Did someone hit you, West?" He wouldn't stand for it with the girls, he wasn't going to stand for it with West either. You didn't hit the people he loved. You just didn't.

"I was in an accident, Ard. Fell down some stairs. Let it be."

"Let me see, West. Did you go to the doctor?" Ardie tugged at West's shirt.

"No. It's just ugly. It doesn't hurt anymore."

Ugly was right -- black and green and yellow and covering West's back, going under his waistband. "Shit, West. You drove with your back hurting like this must have?"

"Well, I couldn't jog here, Ard." West pulled his shirt down. "I'm good. Honest."

"I've got some salve. I'll get you fixed up." He headed toward the bathroom. "You've got to be more careful, West."

"Yeah. I know." West followed him. "I'm really okay."

He found the mason jar of stink ointment that Gerny Smithers made and doled out to everyone in return for favors that was a cure-all for just about everything. It worked, too, even if it did smell to high heaven. "Strip off and I'll fix you up."

"You're kidding, right? I'll stink."

He gave West a look. "You'd rather hurt? It's not like you're trying to impress anyone, right? Besides, it won't be as bad as that time you fell into the manure pile."

"Oh, God. Don't remind me." West laughed, tugged his shirt off. "That was horrific."

"The pigs thought you were one of their own," he teased.

He winced at the sight of West's back in the bright light of the bathroom's bare bulb.

"Well, you set them to rights. Where do you want me, Ard?"

Well, wasn't that a leading question. "I guess that depends on how far down that bruise goes, West."

"To my knees, but I won't subject you to my skinny ass."

"To your knees? Jesus fuck, West!" He bit back his growl. "Your bedroom, West. You can lie on the bed. And it won't be the first time I've seen that skinny ass."

West saluted, winked. "You're getting all riled up, Ard."

"I don't like seeing you hurting, West." And he'd have to be careful, because bruising or not, a mostly naked West *was* going to get him worked up, only not the way West was talking about.

"I know, Ard. I know." West sighed again, shook his head. "I tell you, life isn't the same away from here."

"You could always come back," he murmured quietly, sitting on the bed and waiting for West to get into place.

"No. I have a scholarship, a 4.0. I have to go back."

He nodded and patted the bed. "Come on, West, it's just me. No reason to be shy."

"Yeah, I got nothing you haven't seen."
West stripped down, settling on the bed, all
those bruises exposed for him.

"Jesus, fuck, West. It looks like you lay
down and let someone beat the shit out of you
with a bat."

"Nope. Stairs."

"Yeah, so you said." He got a dollop of
salve and spread it on West's back, working it
gently in.

"Stinky." West took a deep breath, relaxed a
little, shifting. "Good, but stinky."

Ardie chuckled. "No pain, no gain, right?"

"You know it, Ard. So good to be home."

"You don't have anyone back at college to
rub stinky salve into your ass?"

"Not anymore." The words were short,
clipped and hurt. So, apparently Alec, Alex,
whoever, was history.

His hand paused in the small of West's
back. "I'm sorry, West."

"Yeah. Well. Me, too..."

He got another dollop of goo and started to
spread it over West's ass.

West groaned, shivered. "God, that hurts. I
never want to see another set of stairs again."

"I can't believe you drove all that way
hurting this bad. Tell you what, we can spend
the next few days watching movies and stuff --
you can lie on the couch on your stomach." He
was as careful as he could be, moving from
West's ass to the top of his legs.

A soft sigh sounded, West hiding his face in his arms. "Okay."

"I'm sorry." Damn, he didn't want to hurt West, but the salve would make a big difference. "I'm almost done, promise."

"It's not bad. I just... I'm just glad to be here. You're too good to me."

"That's what family's for, yeah?"

"Yeah. Yeah, thank you Ard."

"No problem." No problem at all. Except he could hardly tell West about himself now, could he? Not after he'd just slathered salve all over West's naked ass.

"I'm gonna go wash this shit off my hands."

"'Kay." West sat up, reached for his clothes. "I'm sorry, Ardie."

He frowned. "For what?"

"For... Hell, I don't know. I'm just sorry."

"Well, I'm sorry you got hurt, but I'm not sorry you're home for the summer. I'm damned glad you're here."

He wanted to give West a hug but it felt awkward now, with West naked and the way he felt about his friend.

"Yeah. Yeah, me, too. Go wash. I'll get dressed and meet you in the front room."

"It's a plan." He stopped at the door. "I really am glad you're back, West." He gave West a smile and headed off to wash up.

\*\*\*

West had decided to not take the second summer semester -- he had a job painting houses for the summer, he was enjoying the sun, and he was home. One day, he figured Ard's house wouldn't be that, but right now it was, and it felt good to help out, to see Ard laugh, to just relax and not fight for the best guy, the best grade, the best whatever.

He bought fried chicken and all the fixin's on the way from the site. The sun was shining. The car smelled good. Life was fine and he honked as he pulled up to the little white house. Man, Ardie was going to have to add on. "I brought supper."

Mabel and Tricia came out to meet him, all grins, taking the supper from him. "Ardie said we wouldn't have to cook! He sure does know you."

"That's his job. Did y'all make tea?" He grinned as little Luke came running, legs pumping. He pulled the little kid's meal toy out of his back pocket. "I brought you this."

"Oh, wow!" Luke squealed and grabbed the toy, was halfway up the stairs before he remembered his manners and came running back down, flinging himself at West's legs. "Thanks, Uncle West!"

Ardie came around the side of the house, looking hot and bothered. "Well, I knew from the commotion you had to be home." Ardie gave him a wink.

"I brought chicken. What've you been up to, old man?" He grinned over, grabbed a bottle of Coke and tossed it to Ard.

Ardie caught it and tapped the bottom before opening and downing a good chunk of the drink. "Shifting the hay and straw around -- getting the hayloft ready for the new loads coming in. Damn hot work."

"No shit. I was up on the ladder all afternoon. Got paid, though. Go me."

Ardie grinned and nodded. "You bring home some new movies for us to watch?"

"Yeah. One for the kiddos, too." He was getting good at this uncle thing.

"Cool. They can watch theirs in the front room and we can get a break up in my room." Ardie looked tired out.

"That sounds perfect." The man worked too damn hard.

"You got plans for the weekend, West?"

"Nope. You?"

"I was kind of thinking it'd be nice to grab a few sandwiches, some sodas, and head out to the creek nice and early, settle in for some fishing."

"Works for me, Ard. I need to get as many in as I can before school starts back up."

Ardie nodded. "That's coming up soon enough, isn't it?"

"Three weeks." He sighed, grinned wryly. "Got to order my books this weekend."

"You're going to do us all proud, West." Ardie's arm went around his shoulder. "Come on, let's get our supper on paper plates and eat upstairs." Ardie gave him a smile and then hollered for his sister. "Aggie! You're in charge of the kids."

Aggie's groan made them both grin, hips knocking together as they went up the porch stairs and headed in.

They got the choice pieces of meat and helped themselves to the thick cut fries, Ardie salting his up good. A couple of cans of Coke and they were ready to disappear and be teenagers again, holed up in Ardie's room.

They settled together, flipping channels and eating, just relaxing, being together. Ardie stole back downstairs for a bag of cookies and soon after that they put on the movie. It was always easy and good being with Ard.

It always had been.

"You should come see me at school, Ard. Just for a day or three."

"Yeah? You think I'll fit in with your school people?"

"Sure. We'd have a ball. Go have pizza. Shoot pool. It would be cool." Even if Ard didn't fit in with everybody, it would be good to introduce him around.

Ardie was quiet a moment and then he nodded, smiled. "Okay. Anytime after the crops are in. So after mid-November to be safe. You got a preference?"

"Hmm... You can come after Thanksgiving, but that's finals..." He tilted his head, thinking. "How about right after finals and we'll come back for Christmas together?"

"Oh, that's a great idea -- I can get Christmas for the kids in the city."

"Cool! It's a date then." He grinned over, stole one of Ard's cookies.

"My first," Ard said, giving him a wink.

"Slow bloomer." He winked back, munching away.

Ardie laughed and nodded

They settled, turning on the movie finally, relaxing against the pillows.

Lazy.

Happy.

Home.

At least for a few more weeks.

***

The taxi pulled up in front of West's apartment and Ardie was really glad he'd decided to fly in, letting him and West drive back in West's car. Man, did he feel like a hick, and it only would have been worse in his truck, him trying to navigate roads he didn't know, and damn, there was a lot of traffic.

The taxi driver'd known where he was going, though, and Ardie paid him, waited for his change, and then headed over to the little three-story apartment building. He found West's number and rang the bell.

West opened the door, grinned wide. "Ard! You found me! Come on in!"

The apartment was postage stamp sized. It was all West, though -- a little stark, a little jumbled, computers and books everywhere.

He grinned and couldn't help teasing. "No wonder you're eager to get home when you come."

"Hey! It's better than the dorm and I can work here. Have a seat. You want a Coke?" West was full of energy, bouncing.

"Yeah, sounds good. They were charging three dollars a can on the plane and I figured I could wait."

He sat down on West's bed -- there wasn't a sofa.

West had a little dorm fridge, a coffeemaker and a microwave in the little kitchenette. Mabel would die. The Coke was handed over, West sitting close by. "How was your flight?"

"Freaky. I never did think we were going to get off the ground, but we did. And when we landed again, I breathed."

"I'm glad you came, man. How're all the kids? The baby crawling yet?"

"Shit, she's almost walking. Into *everything*. And Aggie? In the family way. Again." He shook his head. That girl was going to be the death of him.

West looked over at him, wide-eyed. "Hasn't she figured out what causes that?"

"Apparently not. I told her it happens again and I'm going to beat her." She'd looked real scared, though, when he'd suggested that maybe there wasn't room for her and her brood at the farmhouse anymore if it got any bigger, and he had a hunch she was going to be more careful from here on in. Damn, he hoped so, anyway.

"Shit, I'm sorry, Ard. That sucks." West sighed. "How about everybody else?"

"Pretty good. Luke's doing just fine in school -- he needed the challenges it brings. Mabel's getting quieter and quieter. I wish I could afford to bring someone in and take care of stuff for her so she could go do stuff, you know? I suggested community college, she wouldn't hear it."

"Oh, Ard. I wish she would. She deserves to, you both did."

"Aggie did, too. She blew it for all of us, though. Tricia and Luke might make it. If we tighten our belts and start saving up." He was actually relieved he'd had his college decisions made for him. He wasn't sure he was up to the pressure. Or smart enough.

West sighed, shook his head. "Shit, I feel guilty. I'm out here living away and you're working your ass off."

"What? Oh, no, West. This is your dream. You shouldn't feel guilty for living it."

"Well, I don't know if it's my dream, but I'm going to finish. I got a 4.0 again."

"That's great, West! Not that I ever doubted you would. You're the smartest person I know." He beamed over at his friend. West was gonna do them all proud.

"Yeah, I'm trying to get into a program with Dr. Wilson. He does wicked cool programming stuff. It's a lot of work, but I so want to do it."

"I bet you do -- you can do anything you set your mind to, West." Blew them all away in the smarts department, West did. "I don't know if I could take the pressure."

"Well, it's all I do." West stood when one computer beeped, checked the email. "I ought to make you a computer so we can talk."

"That's what phones are for," he teased. God, it was good seeing West again.

"Phones are *so* passé, Ard." West chuckled, winked. "What do you want for supper?"

Ardie snorted and would have swatted West, except he was feeling too lazy to reach for him. "How about something typical of the city, West. When in Rome and all that."

"Pizza. I'll order some in and tomorrow, after my lit paper's turned in? We'll sightsee. Pepperoni?"

"With extra cheese." He settled into a sprawl on West's bed. "Don't let me get in the way of you getting your work done."

"Oh, I won't. I just need to finish that paper and I'm gold." West grabbed the phone, speed dialed. "Hey Marty? 'S West. Yeah. Yeah. I need a pie -- pepperoni and extra cheese. Did you? No shit? Cool. He was hot as fuck in jeans, but a dud in the sack. You're better off rid of him."

Ardie nearly swallowed his tongue.

"Yeah. I know, baby, but he's a bad seed. You know that new guy at the club... Uh... Kevin? Keith? Something... He's more your type."

Ardie cleared his throat and sat up, feeling weird to be listening in on West talking like that.

West smiled over, winked. "Oh, make it a large. I have company. Who? My best friend."

He smiled back at West, that one-sided conversation reminding him that he was in the big city now. He wondered what all West had planned for him.

The conversation ended quickly after that, West coming back to plop down beside him. "On its way."

"Cool. I take it you know the owner? Cook?"

"Cook. He's in my history class."

"Old boyfriend?" West had called the guy baby, after all.

"Oh, God, no. Marty and I aren't compatible. He's just a good friend. He's the secretary of the GLBT organization."

"GLBT organization?" It really was a whole other world.

"Gay, lesbian, bisexual and transgendered. Marty? Is a drag queen." West grinned, looked tickled as all hell. "He's a beautiful woman."

Oh, now, he was swallowing his tongue. His eyes were bugging out, too, he imagined.

"Would you like to meet him?"

"I." He swallowed and nodded. "That was the point of me coming, wasn't it? To meet your friends."

"Yeah. There's a party day after tomorrow, I thought I'd go and show you off to someone."

"Oh, so there is someone special, is there?"

"Not yet, but there's hope. Chris is a little... hesitant."

"I can't imagine someone not jumping at the chance to be with you." There couldn't be bigger fools than him, could there?

"Yeah, but you like me, Ard. You're my friend."

"Well, you wouldn't be interested in someone who doesn't like you, would you?" Of course he'd kind of missed out on the niceties of dating. Didn't figure he'd really ever find out.

"Huh? No. No, of course not. I meant that you're my friend, you're not looking to... I mean. Okay, this is weird..."

He chuckled. "Yeah, it is. We're usually at the farm."

"Yeah, but Marty wouldn't fit in with the cows."

He blinked a moment and then he started to laugh. "Oh, West. I have missed you."

West leaned against him, laughing, eyes dancing.

He had the sudden urge to just lean forward and kiss West, he was close and warm and it would be so easy. It would be easy and right, just to kiss the laughter right off those lips. It would have, but the doorbell rang and West moved, the chance lost.

The story of his life.

*** 

West was having a ball showing Ard around, introducing him to people, sharing his world. Ben's party was just rocking, the wine and beer and music and such flowing free. He'd danced a few times, gotten one nice kiss from Vic in a back corner, spent a lot of time drawing Ard away from the wall.

Ard was currently with Marty and Wilma, another drag queen, blinking and clutching his beer can like it was the only thing keeping him upright. He looked lost, but hot, in a new pair of jeans and a plain black T-shirt. Ard sure did have nice muscles from working on the farm and West knew he wasn't the only one noticing.

He wandered over, smiling wide. "Are you girls being good to him? He's very important to me. I'll be pissed if you scare him."

"Oh, we're taking good care of him, honey." Wilma wrapped one hand around Ardie's arm, the other rubbing across his chest. "Very good care of him."

Ard flushed and gave West a look that was very much deer-caught-in-the-headlights.

"You want to dance with me, Ard?" He figured that would get Ardie a chance to relax and he could see if Ard wanted to bail.

Ardie nodded, not even seeming to think about it. The beer was put on the table behind him and Ardie extricated himself from Wilma's clutches. "Excuse me, ma'am."

He took Ard's hand, pulled him out to the dance floor, moving easy to the music. "You having a good time?"

Ardie moved better than West had expected, finding the rhythm and following it. "It's interesting."

"Is that interesting 'God, I'm going to have to tell my therapist' or interesting 'this is fun'?"

"Therapist? You go to a therapist, West?" It was funny how that seemed to be freaking Ard out more than the whole gay party thing.

"Well, maybe. Sometimes. It's free through the university..." He needed someone to talk to about... everything.

"Oh. Well, I meant interesting as in I'm not quite sure what to make of it interesting."

"Well, everybody's a little wired, being the end of the semester and all. We can go, if you want." The song slowed and so did they.

Ardie kind of glanced around and held open his arms. "I guess we should... And no, we don't have to go -- you're having a great time."

"I can party with these guys anytime, Ard." He stepped closer, moved into Ard's arms, and it was weird -- how not-weird it felt.

Ardie led, shuffling them around in a small circle, and he got a grin. "This reminds me of two-stepping around the front room with Momma. Before Poppa died. Except you're not anything like Momma."

"Nope, I'm taller and skinnier." He smiled, relaxed and easy. "You're a good dancer, Ardie. How come I didn't know that?"

"Because whenever there was a school dance you and I found something better to do."

"Oh. Right." He grinned. "Silly me."

"So where's this Chris person you're hoping to... hook up with?"

"I haven't seen him. He might not have come out." West shrugged. He was having a good enough time without Chris.

"I was hoping to meet him, check him out." Ardie gave him a wink. "Make sure he's good enough for our Westie-Testie."

He chuckled, shook his head. "He's not Mr. Right, Ard. Just Mr. Right Now."

"Is that the way it is here?" Ard asked. "Nobody's looking for that special someone?"

"We're all looking, Ard. We're just not dumb enough to expect it to happen."

Ardie nodded. "I guess I understand that. There's some stuff I don't get, though, West. Like Marty and Wilma. What are those guys dressed as gals looking for, West?"

"Love? Forever? A good hard fuck? Someone to treat them like they're not freaks?"

Ardie stiffened a little. "I didn't say I thought they were freaks, West. I said I didn't understand them. This place is different from where we come from."

"Oh, I wasn't saying you were, Ard. You asked what they were looking for, I told you." He found a real, honest smile. "You're a good man, Ard."

Ardie nodded and relaxed again, tugging him off the dance floor when the music picked up speed again. "But do they want a man or a woman?"

"Marty's gay; Wilma'll sleep with anyone."

"Oh." Ardie nodded and looked around at the party, taking it all in. Ardie didn't seem phased by it all so much as shy.

"Would you like to go somewhere? Have some pancakes and coffee and visit?"

"If you want, West. We haven't had much of a chance to talk, but we can do that at home."

"There's nothing I want more than to just visit with you, Ard." It surprised him, that he meant it.

And it earned him one of Ardie's long, slow smiles that just lit up his best friend's face. "Then let's go get pancakes and coffee and visit."

He squeezed Ard's fingers, nodded. "Sounds perfect."

And it did.

***

They'd packed West's little car up with presents for Aggie and Mabel and the kids and headed back home on the 23rd.

West insisted on doing the driving because it was his car, which just amused the shit out of Ard. But he'd pulled his hat down over his eyes and dozed so he'd be rested in case West changed his mind later.

They were well out of the city when he woke up and he couldn't say he was sad to see it behind them.

He'd enjoyed meeting West's friends. Mostly. He thought it was good to see West in his environment, doing his thing. Made him realize it was just as well he'd never said anything to West about his feelings. He couldn't imagine living in the world West inhabited now and he knew that world was the place West wanted to be.

He'd blown several more opportunities to tell West about himself and figured at this point it didn't much matter.

"You want a Coke?" he asked, reaching to dig around the cooler in the back seat.

"Sure. Thanks." West was humming, thinking, looking good and happy. "You missing home?"

He popped the top on a can and pressed it into West's hand and then did one for himself. "Yeah, believe it or not, I am. I miss all my girls and Luke."

"Yeah. I keep waiting for home to be school and not your house."

Ardie had to smile at that. It was a nice fantasy, West always thinking of the farm as home. "So you don't yet?"

"Nope. When someone says home, it's always you."

Ardie thought about that for awhile. Thought maybe he liked it. A lot. "Well, it always will be. I mean you'll never be turned away, and I guess that makes a place home, doesn't it?"

"I guess so, yeah." West grinned, didn't look disappointed by that. "Yeah."

"So those are some interesting folks you hang out with, Westie-Testie. A far cry from home."

"They're good people, mostly. Good friends."

"Good."

He stared out at the road, watching as the scenery grew more and more familiar, the farms that backed up onto the road like his own. Crops and critters and simple folks. Not better, he imagined. Just different.

"You sure you don't want me to spell you off driving?"

"No, it's okay. I've made the drive in worse conditions."

"But you don't *have* to this time." He just wanted West to know that, to remember he wasn't alone. Not here and certainly not ever. West ever needed for anything, he and the girls were only a call away.

West looked over, looked a little surprised, then nodded. "You want to stop at a Dairy Queen and then we'll switch?"

"Sure, I could eat." He chuckled. "In fact I could fair murder a nice thick burger."

They'd eaten at a dinner party the night before thrown by Wilma, who, for all she --he? -- wasn't picky in the who she'd fuck department, wouldn't eat meat. Vegetarians. Now there was something even stranger than men who dressed like women!

"Oh, hell, yeah. Chili cheese fries, too." West winked, almost bouncing.

He grinned. "Yeah. We can share a peanut buster parfait after, too." Just like old times.

"Sounds perfect." West grinned over. "Much better than tofu cheesecake, huh?"

He shuddered, only exaggerating a little bit. "I appreciate a person's got a set of beliefs, but damn. That wasn't real food."

West chuckled. "I hear you. Soy cheese pizza? Wrong, Ard. Just wrong."

"Oh, I'm glad I missed that one!" He laughed at the expression on West's face.

Damn, he loved being around West. Driving, at West's place, at home. It just felt good.

"You know it." West pulled into the Dairy Queen, killed the engine.

He got out and stretched. "Oh, we needed to stop, switching drivers or not." His ass was rather numb, his knees protesting the cramped quarters of West's little car.

"Uh-huh. I need to piss like a racehorse." West twisted at the waist, one arm up in the air.

Ardie admired the lean form before a gust of wind reminded him it was December. "Come on. My treat."

"Cool." West swatted his ass and then hurried in.

"Bitch," he called out, following, laughing.

"You know it, stud." West grinned, held the door open.

He shook his head, chuckling, took a pinch of West's ass as he went by. Two could play that game.

They were both hungry, ordering burgers and fries, sodas and ice cream. Both of them played, joshing and joking like kids. It felt good, had felt good all week. Being around West made him feel young. It wasn't like he was *old* anyway, but he had responsibilities at home that weighed him down, whereas West made him light, made him young. West stole fries, laughed at all his jokes, just made him feel good.

The food was familiar and good, filling him. The friendship and laughter was better. It wasn't long at all before they were done and he went up to buy the big dessert. Sharing it with West was something of a tradition, the two of them usually low enough on cash they shared everything. At least until the summer West'd gotten his first job.

First job. First boyfriend. First... lover?

It made him sad suddenly and he wasn't sure if he was mourning his own lack in that department or rather that he hadn't been West's first. Of course he would have wanted to be West's first *and* last, but he never would have tied West down to him and the farm, so it was probably just as well.

He paid for the dessert and brought it back to their table with two spoons and lots of napkins.

"You okay, Ard?" West smiled up at him, the look questioning and familiar and warm.

That was his West. He smiled and nodded. "Yeah, West. I do believe I am."

# Chapter Four

West pulled into the driveway and just looked a minute. More than two years he'd been gone and it still looked the same.

He couldn't stay the summer, either. He had to get to Massachusetts, find an apartment, meet his graduate advisor. All that mess. Hell, he shouldn't have come at all, but Mabel was getting married and he couldn't miss it.

He just couldn't.

Little Luke was the first one out the door. Not so little either, he looked like the teenager he soon would be. He was trailed by two little ones, the boy barely on his feet, the girl dragging her brother along. And behind them was Ardie. Looking a little older, looking more than two years older, that was for sure, but a big smile lighting up his face, West's welcome obvious.

"Hey guys. How's it going?" He grinned, waved. Damn. Everyone was... growing up. Even the house was changing, an addition built out the side.

The kids jumped on him, Luke calling him Uncle West, the other two more caught up in the excitement than anything else.

Ardie waited, smiling at him until he was free of kids, and then he was given a bear hug. "Damn, West. You're a sight for sore eyes."

"Yeah? It's been forever, man." He held on for a bit. "How're you holding up with all the wedding preparations?"

"Oh, lord you don't even want to know." Ardie tightened his hold again, only letting go when Mabel cleared her throat.

Ardie grinned. "She wants you to meet the fiancé. This here is Billy Watson -- you remember his older brother was on the ball team with you. He works at the canning factory. Gonna be manager one day, or so he tells me."

Mabel's husband-to-be was almost as small as she was, pimply, and his hand was sweaty, but he seemed earnest enough.

"We're building on an addition," Ardie told him. "Upstairs for Mabel and Billy and their brood, when it comes," he added as Mabel rolled her eyes. "Three rooms downstairs for Aggie and her kids."

West grinned. "Good thing I'm all grown and living on my own, huh? Nice to meet you, Billy."

Ardie laughed. "There's always room for one more, West. And don't you go getting any ideas, Aggie!"

The girl rolled her eyes, looking more settled than he'd ever seen her. Billy just nodded, looking happy to melt back into the background.

He got kisses from Aggie and Mabel. "Thanks for coming," Mabel murmured. "It wouldn't have been the same without you." He thought she was going to say something else but her gaze flicked to Ardie, then back to him, and she just smiled.

"I wouldn't have missed it." Hell, he wouldn't be back until after grad school this time. He'd fought hard for the program he got into, sacrificed anything and everything to get it. He was glad to be here. Now.

"All right, all right, leave the man be." Ardie put a proprietary arm around his shoulders and waved everyone off. "Supposedly the girls' old room is turning into my study, but at the moment, the loft is still the best place to get some peace. What do you say we grab a couple beers and some chips and catch up?"

"Sounds like a plan." He was tired, just worn through, and he could definitely use a long talk and a sit.

"I'll get you the drinks and chips, Bu-Pa. You want anything else?" Luke looked eager to please.

Ardie grinned at him. "Some chocolate bars would be nice and you could grab one for yourself, too."

"Cool!" Luke took off like a shot and Ardie steered him out toward the barn.

"So how's things, West? You look tired."

"Been a long few months, getting ready to graduate." Getting ready to move. To leave. To start another new life.

Ardie nodded. "Long couple years, I imagine, you not getting back before now." Ardie's voice was carefully neutral.

"Yeah." He sighed, looked out into the pastures. He'd spent the last two Christmasses with Chris, loving it, happy as hell. There wouldn't be a third, he guessed.

Luke brought them their stuff and they headed up to the loft, Ardie's ass tight and hot in his jeans right ahead of West.

Once they got settled, side-by-side, looking up at the ceiling, just like old times, Ardie looked over at him. "What happened?"

"With what?" He couldn't play dumb with Ard. They talked on the phone once every few days. Still, he'd try.

Ardie snorted. "You come home with that hangdog look and think I'll just let it pass?"

"It was worth a try, wasn't it?"

"Only if you like participating in useless endeavors, West. Now come on. Talk to me. That's part of why you're here, isn't it?"

"I came to see you, see Mabel's wedding." He looked away, took a deep shaky breath. "I loved him, but Chris, he didn't feel like moving, and then, well, when I offered to stay he didn't feel like that either."

He could hear Chris' voice in his head still. "We're two different people, Wes. You're never going to stop being so... you."

He could hear Ardie's growl now. "Then he couldn't have loved you very well, West, treating you like that. You don't hurt friends like that, you especially don't hurt the ones you love like that." Ardie's hand found his arm, petting gently.

"No, he didn't love me. He... enjoyed me. Liked the fact I cleaned and did his homework and defragged his hard drive."

"Why did you stay with him, West? Why didn't you find someone who'd enjoy you for *you*, not for what you could do for them?" Ardie's hand stayed right where it was, solid and warm, like Ardie himself.

"Because I loved him, Ard." Loved him with all he was. It wasn't enough. He just wasn't enough.

"I'm sorry, West." Ardie tugged him over, resting his head against Ardie's chest, arms going around him. "I'm sorry."

He surprised himself with the tears that filled his eyes, tears he hadn't shed, not even when he'd given Chris his key.

"Sh. Sh, now. It's all right, West. You're home now. Where you're loved. Where you're welcome, yeah? It'll be all right, you'll see." Ardie kept talking, words sliding into each other. It wasn't the words themselves that mattered anyway.

He just nodded, closed his eyes and cried for twenty-seven months of wanting. Wishing. Hoping. And Ardie just held him, murmuring softly, giving him a safe place to fall apart for awhile.

***

Mabel's wedding was in the church and her reception was at the farm. The first had been nice, just what Mabel wanted, the second a bit wild, everyone they knew coming out to help celebrate. Everyone brought chairs and food and gifts. Luckily, it hadn't rained.

Everyone had congratulated Ardie like he was Mabel's father. Plus he'd given her away in the ceremony, which was a bit silly considering she wasn't moving away or anything, but he supposed it cemented the father figure idea in everyone's heads.

He wasn't too sure how to take that. After all, he wasn't even twenty-five yet.

Once the sky got dark and the dancing started, Ardie found West, gave him a wink, and headed for the barn with some beer, some Cokes, and a plate full of sweets.

There wasn't anyone but West he wanted to dance with anyway, so he didn't see any reason to stick around and feel even more like an old man sitting on the sidelines, watching the kids dance. It was bad enough Mabel'd nabbed him for the second dance while Billy waltzed his mom around the field. He *wasn't* Mabel's Daddy. He wasn't Daddy to any of them.

Bu-Pa. Half Bubba, half Pappy, half whatever it was that he was.

By the time he got up into the loft and settled, waiting on West as he listened to the music coming from the front field, he was feeling downright anti-social and grumpy.

"Hey, Ard, you up here?" West blinked, eyes adjusting to the dark.

"Yep. Hiding out from the rabble." He grinned over. Anti-social and grumpy never meant he didn't want to see West.

"Mabel looks happy. You did good." West settled in, dark hair all rumpled.

He chuckled. "All I did was nod and build whatever she asked me to build. Or paid for whatever she asked me to pay for."

"That's more than most brothers would do."

"There wasn't anyone else." And that's why he stepped in as their Daddy.

"I know, Ardie. You're a good man. You always have been."

"Oh, don't go being nice now. I was just sitting here feeling miserable about it. Wishing things were different."

"Yeah." West sighed. "Life dealt you a shitty hand."

"It hasn't been particularly kind, no. On the other hand, things could have been worse. I try not to grouse too much. We're all together. We've got the farm and not a shitload of debt.

I've got the best best friend in the world." He gave West a smile and raised his bottle in a salute.

West gave him a half-smile and a nod. "Thanks, Ard. I sort of suck, though, at the taking care of things thing."

"Oh, I figure we've already got one of those. Two really, if you count Mabel -- and the way she looks out for Momma, you've got to count Mabel. So that position is filled. You're the dreamer. The go out and make the dreams happen dreamer. We needed one of those."

He got a chuckle, a grin. "Yeah, well, we'll see how I do up east."

"You? Are going to blow them away. They're going to wonder how they ever survived without you." He didn't doubt West's brain for a minute.

"I need to have you there, reminding them of that."

He chuckled. "Somehow I think some hick farmer's not going to convince them the way you can. Now, you need me to remind *you* of that? You can call me collect. Anytime, West." He looked West in the eyes. "Anytime."

"I know, Ard. I imagine you'll get them all the time, at least at first."

"You're going to do great, West. I'm not just blowing sunshine up your ass either, I truly believe that. You were made for this." Just like he was made to farm and take care of his family. It was why maybe it was a good thing, he'd never told West his true feelings.

"Yeah." They were quiet for a long bit, sitting and drinking, then West looked over. "Talked to my mom the other day. They bought a house in Florida. They're retiring."

"No shit? Finally settling in one place?" Florida. Heh. He was selfish enough to wonder if that meant he'd be seeing even less of West.

"So she says. They tried to make it to graduation, but they couldn't, so I didn't go."

"Aw, West, I'm sorry. You know I would have come if I could. But between getting the crops in, putting the addition on the house and Mabel's wedding, it just didn't work."

West grinned. "Got me some time to get shit done, Ard. Hell, I was crashing at Marty's anyway."

He winced. That sure wasn't the graduation celebration he would have wished for West.

"Well, I'll make it to the next one and we'll make sure you have a big todo."

"That sounds like a good plan, Ard. We'll celebrate it in style."

"Yeah. I don't think I know anyone who went to after college before."

"Well, that's where the money is." West shrugged. "It'll be three years of hell and then the good money."

"I thought you liked schooling?"

"This ain't school, Ard. This is research and eighty hours a week work for free."

"Well, that sounds like a good deal for the guys you're working for. Is it worth it? Being the dog for them for three years?"

"Adam Harrington? Guy I know from there? Made six figures in two years."

"Wow, you'll be made, West. Cool." He grinned. "And you like the work, yeah? Playing computer games?"

"Making them, Ard." West chuckled. "And yeah, yeah I do. I love it."

"Well, it's all Greek to me, West." He grinned and nodded at the plate of goodies. "Pass me a slice of that pie, will you?"

"Yep." West handed it over. "I'm leaving my car here, Ard. It's in good shape, low mileage. You'll get use out of it."

"I can't pay you for it, West. You sure you don't want to drive it up?"

"I didn't ask you to pay for it, asshole. I'll just need a ride to the airport."

He whapped West for the asshole comment. "Well, Mabel's been wanting a car to do the groceries and her errands and stuff. It'll make a right pretty wedding present. Thanks, West."

"You're welcome." West stole a couple chips, grinned over. "That was easier than I thought it would be."

He snorted. "You played me, did you? Made sure I was liquored up and in the middle of all this wedding madness before you made your move."

"You know it. You'd better just pray your ass is safe." West's eyes were just *twinkling*.

"Oh, now you're telling me you've gifted my sister with a lemon?"

"Never. I'm telling you this wedding madness is contagious. I'll call home one day and find you with a son on the way."

"Me?" He laughed and shook his head. "No way. You've got to like girls for that to happen, West." And just like that, he'd finally told West. No plans, no going over the conversation in his head, he just blurted it out.

West blinked over, tilted his head. "You telling me what I think you're telling me, man?"

"Well, I don't know what you're thinking, but what I'm telling you is if I were to date, it wouldn't be with a girl."

"Well, I'll be damned." West grinned. "Do you have someone, then?"

"Oh, hell, no." He shook his head. There wasn't really anyone he could have, and besides, his heart was already set on West, now wasn't it.

"No? That's a shame, Ard. You deserve to be happy, more than anyone I know."

"I am happy, West." And he was. For the most part. He had dreams and wishes that were just going to have to stay dreams and wishes, but on the whole he was happy.

"Oh. Okay." West nodded, looked uncomfortable for a second, then grinned. "I can hear Mabel laughing."

He was quiet a minute, trying to hear what West did. He shook his head. "I can't hear anything over the music."

"It was cute."

Ardie snorted, but let West change the subject. He wasn't sure why West seemed upset that he was gay, too. Unless West thought he was just copying him or something.

"You'll have to send me pictures of the wedding and shit, so I can show the guys I meet."

"You'll have to talk to Mabel about that. She's in charge of all that shit." He took a long swig of his beer. "As of now, I am officially weddinged out. Unless Aggie decides to find someone to make an honest woman of her."

"That would mean just picking one."

He laughed and then poked his finger at West. "That's my sister you're talking about, bub."

"Yeah, yeah. I know." West grinned. "I guess I should be sorry, huh?"

"Nah. It's only true." He grinned and finished off his beer. He was starting to feel pretty easy in his bones.

West drank a little slower than he did, but looked like he was moving as slow.

He popped the top off another beer. "So what's it like?" he asked.

"What's that, Ard?"

"You know. With guys." He waved his hand vaguely in the air and decided he should have waited until he'd finished this beer before starting this conversation, so he downed half of it.

"It's good. I like sex. A lot. Some of the games and shit? Sorta weird and not hot. But just making love? It's great."

"Games? Weird?" Shit, he'd been talking about kissing and getting off. There was weird shit and games, too?

"Yeah, people are into all sorts of things, Ard. Some of it's good, some ain't."

"Do I even want to know?"

"No, I don't think so. The basics, though? They're sweet."

"Good." He liked to think of West as getting something sweet, something good. He didn't ask, though, was happy just assuming that that's what West went for.

Though, why then would West know about the other stuff? Well, because he was a smart guy.

Ardie frowned, logic getting lost somewhere.

Maybe it was the beer.

"Yeah." West stretched out. "I keep wondering when I'll stop missing him."

"Well, it hasn't been that long, has it? Not to depress you or anything, but I miss you every day, whether I saw you yesterday or it's been two years." He had his hand back on West, patting his friend's leg.

"You're too good to me." West smiled over, eyes warm.

"That's what friends are for, right?" He squeezed West's leg, smiling wide, feeling fine.

"Yeah. Am I good for you, Ard?"

"You think I'd want to keep you around if you weren't, West?"

"I hope not."

"You're my best friend, West. I'd like you around more. Hell, I'd like you around lots." He squeezed West's leg again.

God, it was just like back at West's place that Christmas. They were close enough all he'd have to do was lean in a little...

West blinked over at him. "You'd get tired of me, Ard. Everyone does, eventually."

He snorted. "I haven't in... damn how long has it been, West? Since the second damned grade and we were inseparable until you went off to college." Get tired of West. As if.

He got a grin. "A long, long time."

"Well, there you go. I got staying power. Or you do. Or maybe it's a combination."

"Could be. Think it's you, though. You're the solid one."

He grinned, winked. "You mean stuck in the mud and boring."

"No." West shook his head. "You've never bored me, Ard."

"Cool." He beamed at West, feeling just fine. Just fine.

"Yeah." West started chuckling. "Way cool."

"You're drunk," he noted.

"Yep. So're you."

"Yeah, just a little." He chuckled and leaned against West, glad they were already lying down because he wasn't sure he'd still be standing.

"I might have had a few."

"A couple three."

He nodded and giggled. Fucking giggled. Yep. Drunk.

West snorted, laughing hard. "Oh, you are the best thing in my life, Ardie."

"Ditto, Westie-Testie. Ditto."

The best damned thing ever.

# Chapter Five

Brian chuckled, reached over and goosed him. "Man, Wes-baby. You? Grew up in the middle of fucking nowhere. It's like a movie. I love it."

West grinned over, daring a quick kiss at the stoplight. "I can't wait for you to finally meet Ardie, B. He's something else."

"Oh, hell, baby. I feel like I know him already, all the time we spend on the phone while you're at work." He chuckled and nodded. The complaint was a familiar one. Three years they'd been working different schedules -- B on nights at the hospital, him on sixteen-hour days at the office. Still, they were managing.

"Yeah, yeah. You sure didn't mind the car I bought you for your birthday..."

Brian chuckled. "No, I didn't, and you have to work, just like I do, baby. I just miss your tight little ass."

"You watch that mouth, Dr. Hawkes. These folks are decent."

"Then I'd better get it all out now, hadn't I?"

"Too late. We're here!" He pulled up to the house, grinned wide.

Luke showed up first, Aggie's two girls and the latest wee one in tow, Mabel, hands full of flour, not far behind them. And bringing up the rear, looking just the same and all smiles, was Ardie.

They got out of the rental car, Brian's teeth white and shining in his dark face, his lover just fine in jeans and tennis shoes. "Hey, y'all! This is Ardie's brood. Ard? I brought Brian to meet you."

"About time, West." Ardie grinned and gave him a bear hug before turning to Brian. "Well, now, let's meet you in person, Brian."

Brian shook Ardie's hand, grinned. "Man, it's nice to see you, finally."

West grinned, watching the two people he loved best in the world in the world meet. It was about time.

Ardie was giving Brian a good long look and Mabel nudged him. "I recognize that look," she whispered. "Billy got that look."

He chuckled, kissed her cheek. "Brian's a good man. He'll pass."

She gave him a serious look. "He's just glad you're happy, West."

He nodded. "I am, Bell. I am. He's it for me." Funny, too, he'd taken a classmate who'd ODed into the emergency room and met this beautiful, smiling senior resident and bam! Instant chemistry.

The smile she gave him was a little sad, he thought. "Good for you, West."

Ardie turned to him then, arm going around his shoulder, one already around Brian's. "Well, come on in. You haven't even seen the place since the addition was finished, have you?"

"I haven't. It's been a hundred years, Ard. You're looking good for an old man." One of his hands went around Ard's waist.

"Well, that's good to know -- I worked hard to make sure I didn't need my walker this visit."

Brian chuckled. "Damn, physical therapy's getting better and better."

Ardie laughed and led them in, showing them around. "We did the work ourselves. Bit of help from the neighbors."

"It's beautiful, Ard. Y'all did a great job."

Ardie beamed and gave him another hug. "Damn, West, it's been too long."

"Next time you'll have to come to Seattle, Ard. We're buying a house. You'll have to come see."

"A house? All the way out in Seattle? Well, congratulations, West. I'm happy for you."

Brian chuckled. "Thanks. I'm not sure Wes has even seen all of it. I did the shopping for it."

West reached over, popped Brian's ass. "Stop it, turkey."

"You been busy, West?" Ardie watched their byplay with a fond smile.

"A little."

Brian snorted. "He leaves the house at six a.m., comes home ten at night, on the nights I'm off."

"Well, you can't fault his work ethic." And coming from Ardie, that was quite the compliment.

"No. Or his brilliance." Brian's dark eyes met his and West blushed dark, pleased all through.

Ardie nodded, looking satisfied. "Smartest man I know."

"Y'all stop it." He rolled his eyes, cheeks feeling like they were on fire.

"Modest, too." Brian chuckled. "And cute."

Ardie nodded. "He's not perfect, though. You know that, right?"

Brian snorted. "He works eighteen hours a day, he can't cook, he drinks seven pots of coffee a day, and can't dance worth a damn. I know."

"And you're still with him. Good." Ardie nodded again, looked happy.

"Well, yes. I love the skinny fool."

West was just floating.

Yeah. Yeah, this was...

Perfect.

"Good. Let me get the beer." Ardie's voice was gruff and he headed off.

Everybody sort of wandered off and West turned to Brian, stepping close. "I'm glad you came, love."

Brian nodded, pulled him in for a kiss. "Wes-baby, this is your family. I wanted to come."

He wrapped his arm around Brian's shoulders, holding on. "Thank you."

He'd never been so happy. Ever.

\*\*\*

Ardie'd thought that meeting West's true love was going to be hard. And he had to admit it hadn't been easy, but it hadn't been that hard either. Not after he'd seen the way Brian looked at West like West hung the moon.

This man was someone who loved West the way West deserved, who was supporting him in his dreams. Who didn't have a farmhouse full of responsibilities to keep him from being what West needed.

And dammit, Ardie liked the man.

Of course that didn't mean he wasn't pleased as punch when he went down for a snack around two am to find West already there, raiding the fridge ahead of him. "You better not have taken the last piece of peach pie, Westie-Testie."

"Nope. Potato salad." West gave him a happy grin, handed the pie over. "Brian's asleep, but my stomach was talking to me."

He laughed. "I don't think that was your stomach, it was Mabel's food."

West laughed. "She's amazing. She ought to start a catering business."

"Oh, go ahead and suggest that to her. You should have seen the strip she tore off Billy for it."

"Why? It's good money, good work."

"Something about having to do it at home and not wanting to have to do it full time as work, too. Maybe she'll listen to you -- you're special."

They settled at the table, West grinning over. "Yeah, well, Brian and I could maybe invest in her business. We have some capital, a little."

His jaw dropped a little. "Well, that makes you extra special, then." He shook his head. "You don't have to do that, though, you know. Billy's management position came through and Aggie's managed to hold down a job for the last year or so. We're doing fine."

"It's a business decision, Ard. Brian and me? We have a little interest in a book store, a bit with a dot com. It's not charity."

He frowned. "Just how much of an investment are you talking here, West? Because we're doing okay, but we don't have money to start up something like that."

"Brian and Mabel are chatting about it, Ard."

"Oh." It wasn't that he didn't mind not having been included, he was just surprised Mabel hadn't said anything. Aggie was going to have to really step up to the plate around the house if Mabel got to working full time.

West shrugged. "It felt more... official if Brian talked to her. You know?"

He nodded. "I'm just surprised is all." He gave West a wry grin. "I've been the family patriarch long enough, the one everyone turned to for everything, that it just startled me a little, them talking about this without me."

"Brian's a go-getter, Ard. He didn't even think to talk to you first." West sighed, squeezed his hand. "Have you thought about maybe finding a home for your mom? Letting professionals take care of her?"

"That doesn't seem right, West, having strangers look after her. We take care of our own." He squeezed West's hand back. He couldn't do that to her; he was pretty sure Mabel couldn't, either.

West sighed, shook his head. "You all deserved better."

He shrugged; he'd made his peace with it a long time ago. The hardest dream to give up had been West himself, but now even that one was put to bed, with Brian in the picture. "You've got to play the hand you're dealt, West. I think we've done pretty good with the cards we got." Maybe it wasn't perfect, but they were a family.

"Yeah. I'm glad you're happy, Ard."

He nodded. "I know, because I'm glad you are, too. You and Brian seem really tight. You deserve someone who looks at you like he does."

"He's a good man. Sometimes I can't believe I found him." West smiled, shrugged. "I love it here, but it wasn't where I'm supposed to be."

"You'd have been bored out of your mind." He nodded. He knew that. One of the reasons maybe why it wasn't too hard to meet Brian.

"Bored's a strong word. I'm just meant for a bigger place."

"Bigger things." He nodded. He knew that, too.

"Different things." West looked a little sad. "I still miss you."

He reached out, touched West's cheek. "Oh, West. I miss you, too. Every day, you know."

West nodded, smiled. "I know."

He let his hand fall away before he started caressing. "It helps, though, knowing you're so happy with Brian."

"Yeah, I am. I love him."

"Good. Really good." He squeezed West's hand and went back to his pie.

"I want you to come out, see my house, when we get settled."

He nodded. "After the crops are in? I can do that."

"Excellent. We'll have a blast -- go exploring."

He chuckled. "Sounds good. You think you'll be able to take the time off for me?" He couldn't help teasing, how many times had he called and gotten Brian, being told West was at work?

"I'll take it, for you, Ardie-Pardie." West winked over. "I can always telecommute."

"Oh, you're going to make me blush." He winked back, chuckling.

Their laughter filled the room, low and happy and familiar.

"Well, I'm glad you came to visit, West. Glad you brought your man, too. You're both welcome back anytime, yeah? I like to think you still think of this as home in some way."

West smiled. "In some ways, Ard, this place will always be home."

"It'll always be here for you, buddy. Long as one of us has breath in us you've got a place."

His fingers were squeezed. "Thank you, Ard. You know I wouldn't give for you."

"I know." He smiled down at their fingers. In another time, under different circumstances, they might have been lovers.

They sat for a minute, then West stood, put their plates in the sink. "Come on, Ard. It's late."

He nodded. "Go on up, I should check on the kids, make sure everyone's where they're supposed to be."

"Okay. Night, Ard." West hugged him tight, kissed his temple. "Sleep well."

"You, too, West."

He grinned until West had left and then his smile faded.

Yeah, meeting Brian hadn't been as hard as he was expecting.

It hadn't been easy either.

\*\*\*

They were having a cookout -- the grill blazing, steaks smelling delicious. The kids were playing in the backyard, all the grownups were drinking beer and laughing, everyone happy, teasing.

Brian was having a ball, making friends with the kids, with Mabel. And Ardie? Well, Brian just kept grinning, saying they needed to find Ard a nice boy to play house with.

Ardie overheard him once and shook his head. "I've already got a houseful, Brian."

"Yeah, Ardie, but your bed isn't full." Brian had laughed, clapped Ard on the shoulder.

Ardie blushed hard, chuckling. "Maybe I just don't kiss and tell."

West hooted, clapped. "Are you going out walking, Ardie-Pardie?"

Ardie's blush got deeper and he ducked his head. "Hell, no, West."

God, it was fun to laugh, to be together and relaxed.

"Ardie's gonna die a virgin," said Agnes.

"Don't be a bitch, Aggie. If he does, it's to make up for you." West wouldn't let her run Ard down, giving the tease right back.

"West!" Ardie shook his head, but he was grinning, too.

He winked over, Mabel toasting him, clinking their beer cans together.

"Least ways I know how to have fun," pouted Agnes.

"Aggie." Ardie's voice was soft, but he gave his sister a look and she piped down.

Brian chuckled. "You come up and stay with us, Ard. We'll show you a good time."

"I don't know whether to look forward to it or worry about it." Ard gave him a wink.

West snorted. "Both, of course. It'll be something to write home about."

"As long as no one gets knocked up."

Mabel nearly choked on her beer.

West howled, laughing so hard he toppled from his chair and against Brian's legs.

"Careful, baby, it wasn't *that* funny."

"Uh-huh."

Ardie was looking pleased with himself. "No one laughs at my jokes like West does."

"Ardie's the funniest man on earth." West didn't get why *everybody* didn't think so.

"Thank you, my friend. At least someone thinks so."

West stole a long drink of Brian's beer. "You're welcome, Ardie-Pardie."

Ardie bunched up a napkin and tossed it at him.

Brian caught it, chuckled. "Now, now. No abusing my man."

That just made them all laugh harder.

"You get good steak like this up in Seattle?" Ardie asked. "Or are they all tofu eating vegetarians?"

"There's all sorts of good food -- the seafood? Nice." West grinned over. "There's nothing like a good steak cooked outside, though."

"I hear you get lots of rain out that way, too. And damp."

Mabel chuckled. "You trying to talk him back home, Ardie?"

"Just reminding him about the good things here."

West grinned, leaning closer as Brian rubbed his neck. "Yeah, talk to me when it's eighty thousand degrees here in August."

"Ah, baking weather." Ardie just grinned. "That's when you sit in the creek and let the fish nibble your toes."

Brian chuckled. "Wes doesn't sit and relax, Ardie. It's not his style."

"No? He used to. Maybe he just needs the smell of hay to do it."

"I just got busy." West snorted, shifting a little. "I'm capable of relaxing."

"You just never do from what I understand," murmured Ardie. "I hear that's bad for your heart."

Oh, someone had been talking to Brian just a little too much. He reached out, pinched Brian's leg. "Don't listen to him. He's a worrywart."

"And a doctor. And with you all the time. Who else am I supposed to listen to, West? You gotta take care of yourself."

Aggie was rolling her eyes. "Come on, Ardie. You aren't *everyone's* father, you know."

West looked at Aggie, tilted his head. "Nope, he's not. Of course, lucky for your kids he tries to be, otherwise they'd have none at all."

"You see, Brian, this is how I *know* West is family -- he and Aggie go at it like brother and sister." Ardie was chuckling.

Brian nodded, kept rubbing and massaging. "They definitely go after it."

West snorted and grinned. "Just telling the truth."

"Oh, fuck you, West. I'm tired of your cracks."

"Agnes Caroline Bodine, you apologize this minute."

"You're not my father either, Ardie."

"I am the man of this house, though, and I won't have you talking to people that way. You made your bed, you need to learn to lie in it."

She glared, but muttered an apology to him.

"No sweat, Ags." West glared right back. *Fucking user.*

"Play nice," murmured Ardie.

Aggie stood and curtseyed. "Yes, Bu-Pa, Sir." Then she stomped off, slamming the door behind her.

"She's cute when she flounces." Brian's voice was light, teasing, tickled, diffusing the tension.

"I imagine that's how she managed to get knocked up twice," murmured Mabel.

"Mabel!" But Ardie was snickering.

"I kept telling Ard to buy her a little motorcycle so that she'd stop having reasons to get into back seats, Bell." *Ard was gonna kick his ass.*

"You better behave, Westie-Testie, or I'll pull out the photo albums to show to your man."

"Don't you dare." *He'd been a dorky looking kid.*

Brian hooted. "Oh, man. What do I have to pay?"

"I think Mabel knows where they all are," Ardie said, then added helpfully. "And I think maybe she owes you one or two, Brian."

Mabel giggled and got up, heading for the house.

"Bell! You *traitor*!"

Brian held him, kept him from going after her. "Come on, baby. I want to see everything." Soft lips brushed his ear, so warm. "I want to know all of you."

"Oh." He relaxed, distracted, derailed.

Ardie chuckled. "You sure have his number, Brian."

"Years of practice, Ard. It just took practice."

Mabel came back with a box full of old photo albums and Ardie laughed. "Oh, there's some winners in there."

"One day, Ardie-Pardie. One day, I'll pay you back."

He meant it, too.

"I'll be waiting -- you know where to find me."

\*\*\*

Phone calls in the middle of the night were never a good thing and Ardie stumbled into the hall, grabbing it off the receiver. "Hello?"

"A...a...ard?"

"Shit, West? What's the matter?" He leaned against the wall, heart thumping.

"There... Brian was... There was a..." West's voice trailed off, soft sobs sounding.

"Oh, God, West. Something happened to Brian?" Shit. He rubbed his forehead, hand unsteady. "You need me to come, West?"

"No. No, his family wants him b...buried in Philadelphia. I'm... I'm taking him there. I... I just needed to tell you."

"Dead? Oh, West. I'm sorry, buddy. So damned sorry." Shit. Shit. Brian had been everything to West. The light of his fucking life. "You sure you don't want me to come?"

"I'm sure. I am. I just..." West made a soft little noise. "I've been at the hospital for hours. There was a shooting -- some drug thing, they think. He never woke back up. I talked to his mom and then told them to turn off the machines. He just sort of... stopped breathing."

"Oh, West. Shit. I'm sorry. That had to have been just awful. You going to be all right? You need *anything*?"

"I need Brian back."

"I wish I could do that for you, West." He truly did. He knew how devastating the death of a loved one was, had seen what it had done to his Momma, losing his Poppa so early. Seven years West and Brian had been together, maybe more. Christ.

"Yeah, me, too. I'm sorry I woke you. I just needed to hear a friendly voice."

"I wish I was there for you, West. Wish I could help you out."

Mabel came down along the long hall from her and Billy's wing. He put his hand over the mouthpiece and whispered, "Brian was killed."

Her eyes went wide, her hand to her mouth.

"Mabel offers her condolences, too, West. We all really liked Brian."

"Yeah. Yeah, I know. He loved you all."

"He was a good guy, West. You did all right. Had some good years together, too, yeah?" He slid down the wall, cradling the phone against his shoulder.

"Yeah. Guess I wasn't meant for forever. He was too good for me."

"No, West, that's not the way it works. You're a good man and you deserved him. You made him happy."

"How's everybody there? I... I was thinking I'd fly down for a day or two, just to say hello after... Before I came back here."

"That sounds good, West, real good. You come home and let us hold you. Let us help make it better."

"Just a day or two. I'll call and let you know when my flight comes in?"

"That'll work, West. You know we're here for you."

"I know. I need to make some more calls, Ard. I'll talk to you later."

"Call when you need to, West. Call collect, whatever. And you take care of yourself. Okay?"

"Yeah. Goodbye Ard." The click seemed loud, so odd and final.

Damn.

He reached up to hang the phone up and leaned his head against the wall, fretting, worrying about his best friend. About the man he loved.

\*\*\*

West walked through the airport without seeing a thing. He kept his sunglasses on and just headed to the baggage claim on the lower level. Ard would find him or not.

It didn't matter.

Ardie showed up before his bags did, arm going around his shoulders, squeezing him against the solid body. "Hey, West."

"Hey." He nodded up, eyes not quite meeting Ard's. "Thanks for picking me up." He wasn't in a place to drive.

"No problem, West. How're you holding up?"

"I'm okay." He really was. The doctor had given him a bottle of Xanax and told him to take them. They made things easier. Not good. Nothing was going to be good again. But easier.

"We'll take care of you a couple days, West. You can just let go."

He nodded, grabbing his suitcase when it came through. "How is everybody? Bell have her baby yet?"

"Oh. I haven't told you yet, have I?" Ardie gave him a sad look. "She lost the baby, West." He winced, head drooping further. He shouldn't have come here. Bad news followed him everywhere. "She lost it about a week before you called. I didn't... well, I didn't think you needed to hear it that night."

"I'm sorry. I shouldn't have come, Ard."

"What? Of course you should. You're family, West. You're hurting. This is where you should be."

Ardie guided him out to where the truck was parked. He put his suitcase in the back, climbed up without a word. An hour and some until they got to Ard's house, and then he could just go to bed for a while.

Ardie waited until they were out on the highway and then one hand slid over to rest on his leg and squeezed. "So what do you need, West?"

"I don't know. I just don't want to go home yet."

"Well, you can stay as long as you like, West. You know that." Ardie squeezed his leg again.

He nodded. "Thank you. Can we stop for a can of Coke, please? I'm thirsty."

"Sure. There's the Dairy Queen or Watson's Diner? We can have a burger or something, just sit for awhile."

"Okay. I can do that." He looked down at his wrist; he was wearing Brian's watch. It had been a graduation gift. It said, "To our beloved son, Dr. Wilson."

"Dairy Queen's more impersonal, Watson's got better food."

"Watson's is more private. Stop there." He didn't want to talk to anyone.

"Whatever you want, West."

Ardie made the rest of the trip in silence, hand occasionally squeezing his leg. It wasn't all that long before they were pulling into Watson's little parking lot. He felt like he was wrapped in cotton wool, like he was dreaming. Like he would wake up in a minute with Brian laughing, teasing him, telling him he worked too hard.

He was still sitting in his seat when Ardie opened the passenger door. "I can just get you a can of Coke if you want, West."

"No. No, sorry. Sorry. I'm coming." He slid down, gave Ard a half-smile. "I'm a little dazed."

"Hell, West, I can't say I blame you." Ardie closed the door for him, led him on into the diner and a booth at the back. "Pair of Cokes to start, please," Ardie called out to the waitress as they passed her by.

He sat with his back to the restaurant, watched Ardie sit. "Thank you for sending the flowers. His mom liked them." The church had been packed. Everyone loved Brian.

Everyone.

"What about you?" Ardie asked.

"They were very pretty." He didn't even remember them. Helen had mentioned some had come.

"West... it's me -- Ardie. Talk to me, buddy."

"I..." He looked down at his hands, at the matching rings -- one on his index finger, one on his ring finger. "I don't know what to say. The funeral was packed, was beautiful. The memorial service at the house was beautiful. His headstone is marble. He's buried next to his grandparents." Rotting and dead and buried in the ground. His ass was going to be cremated, no question. Rotting was disgusting.

"How are you, West? Not how was the funeral, where is he buried. How are *you*?"

"I wish it had been me instead."

Ardie made a noise, but didn't say anything, hand reaching over to squeeze his.

"I had to identify the body. He was pale, but he didn't look dead, just like he was sleeping." He'd been shot in the chest and the sheet had covered that. There'd just been this dipped in bit, that's all.

Ardie winced. "Oh, hell, West, that must have been horrible."

"I guess it was." It wasn't the worst part. He was pretty sure he hadn't found the worst part yet.

The waitress came with their Cokes and Ardie sat back.

"You boys know what you want yet?"

"West? You hungry? When was the last time you ate?"

"I don't remember. Friday?" He didn't even know what today was.

"Jesus, West. We'll have two specials, ma'am."

The bubbles in the Coke felt good, sort of sharp in his throat. Cleansing.

"How're you, Ard?"

"Honestly? I'm worried. My best friend looks and sounds like a ghost. His heart got ripped out and I can see him bleeding, but I don't know what to do to help him."

"Don't worry." He unwrapped the silverware the waitress had brought. "I'm just trying to cope."

"It's okay to ask for help with that, yeah?"

"Yeah." He put his napkin in his lap. "There's all sorts of things to do. There's going to be a trial. I need to go to his locker at the hospital. I need to make a list."

"We'll help you sort everything out, West. Mabel's good with lists."

He nodded, then shook his head. "I don't want to bother her."

"It won't be a bother, West. She'll be happy to help, to have something to do."

"Brian was excited about the baby. Bought it a little stuffed rabbit." Brian was an only child, like him.

"He was a good man, West. We all liked him."

He knew that. He knew how good Brian was. How unfair it all was. How wrong it was. How Brian had a long life in front of him. He knew. West nodded. "I know. He felt comfortable with you."

"I don't know what to say, West. I'm sorry it happened. I know you're hurting. I'm here for you."

"Thank you." He looked at the table, then up at Ard. "If it's any consolation I was terrified to come see you after your dad died. I didn't know what to say either."

"I was so glad you were there, though. It made everything seem... I don't know, like it was going to be all right because you were still there."

He reached out, squeezed Ard's hand, nodded because telling Ardie the truth wouldn't help.

Ard wasn't going to make it all right. Nothing would. Ever.

# Chapter Six

Ardie checked his watch and tried not to fret.

Noon on Sunday and West still hadn't called.

It wasn't like either of them had ever said they had a standing phone call at ten a.m. on Sundays, that's just how it had come about.

West would call and they'd talk. Sometimes for a couple minutes, sometimes a couple hours. But West hadn't missed a Sunday morning since he'd gone back home after Brian's funeral. He heard Mabel and the kids come back from church and escaped up into his room to do his fretting in private.

Finally, at dusk, the phone rang, West's voice sounding raw and rough on the hello.

"Hey, West. You're sounding like it's been a long day." He was worried and relieved together.

"Yeah. Been working hard. Trying to get a cold. How's things there?"

"Good. Good. Aggie's fixing to whelp another one. Mabel's hired on a full-time order taker/accountant. There's talk of opening a shopfront rather than just the private parties.

And you work too hard, West. A man needs to sleep, enjoy life a little."

"Good for Bell. Tell her I'm proud." He heard something -- a lighter, maybe, then West sighed. "Take Aggie and get her fixed, Ard."

He let the crack about Aggie go; it wasn't anything he hadn't thought himself when he'd first heard. "Are you smoking again, West? Those things'll kill you."

"Promises, promises. How's Luke doing? Did he get the check I sent him?"

"Yeah, he called yesterday, said you'd sent him some spending money. I suggested strongly you meant him to spend it on stuff like food and school supplies. He said he was gearing up for mid-terms. He sounded a bit stressed. Just like you." Luke was smarter than anyone of them. Ardie knew he'd do well, just like West had done.

"Good boy. I'll send him a little more in a few weeks."

"You're going to spoil him."

"He's a good kid, Ard. I don't have anyone to spend it on."

"He is, and sure you do, West -- yourself." Ardie settled into his chair. "Speaking of yourself, how are you really?"

"Working hard. I have two projects going out this month. Did I tell you I sold the house? The movers are coming next week."

"Yeah, you did. I suggested you come back home." Although to be fair, he made the suggestion once a month or so. He always left it a casual suggestion, he didn't want to push, but West wasn't taking care of himself, and it worried him.

"I found a little apartment in the same building I work in. It'll be convenient."

He nodded. Really, he'd given up on hoping West might come home one day to stay. "Sounds good, West."

"Yep. I sold both the cars, tons of stuff. Gotta love eBay."

"Did you keep anything?" He wasn't sure selling off everything that was going to remind West of Brian was a good idea. On the other hand, West seemed to be having a hard time. Still.

"Three computers. Clothes. Some books. The microwave. Necessary stuff."

"Did it help?" he asked softly.

"No." West took another drag. "But he's everywhere, Ard. Every fucking place I go, he's there."

"You've got to give it time, West. Let it ease, let it heal." He wished he could take that pain away, make things easier for his best friend.

"It's been months, Ard. Hopefully moving will help."

"I hope so, buddy. I sure as hell hope so." It killed him, knowing how much West was hurting. And he had to figure West wasn't letting him know just how bad it really was.

"Yeah. Me, too." West sighed. "My phone number won't change, though. You'll still be able to find me."

"You're never home," he pointed out with a chuckle.

"That's why I have a cell phone, doofus."

He chuckled. "I read they cause cancer." He loved teasing West.

"That and every other fucking thing known to man, Ard."

"Yeah? Even pig shit?"

"I'm not eating pig shit, Ardie, and it wouldn't surprise me."

He laughed. It had been awhile since West had joked this easily with him.

West chuckled. "You need anything with all those babies coming and going?"

"A house on the other side of the farm." He grinned. "Nah, we're good. Mabel's store's just taking off and those that aren't helping out with the farm are helping out there. Even Aggie's stepped up, running the cash."

"You mean she can count?"

"Don't be a bitch, West. She's trying."

"Ard. She's a fucking user. She's a shitty mother, a worse sister. The only thing she manages is to have attractive children and she can't take care of them without you."

"Her father died when she was twelve, West. It was a hard time for all of us. She... made some stupid choices. And she's my *sister*." It was an old argument.

"Yeah. I know. Not my business, anyway." He could almost see West shrug. The man's tolerance since Brian's death was non-existent.

"Sure it is; you're family, West, just like she is. Families have good and bad in them, yeah?"

"Yeah. You're a good guy, Ardie."

"Oh, yeah, a real saint." He snorted.

"Yeah. You take care of your whole family. Brian saved lives. I? Make video games. Go me."

"Okay, stop that. Right now. You're a good man, West."

"I'm a cerebral moron who makes first-person-shooters and makes a fortune doing it."

He hated it when West got down on himself like this. It happened all too often since Brian had died. "Don't make me come up there and whup your ass, Westie-Testie."

"I'm shaking in my shoes, Ard." West chuckled. "Petrified."

"Bitch." He said it fondly. God, he loved that man and it was killing him, how hard West was taking this, how he wasn't getting over Brian's death.

"You know it." West sighed. "I'd better go, Ard. I'm going to pack a little and take a nap."

"Okay, West. You take care of yourself, buddy. I mean it."

"I do. Y'all be good."

"You, too, West. You, too."

He heard West click off and slowly hung up the phone.

Damn, he worried about West.

***

West pulled up to the farm the day before Mrs. Bodine's funeral in a sleek rental car that looked completely out of place with the lines and lines of pickups.

Still, it looked like Ard was doing okay. He knew Bell was, the business rocking. God, he hadn't been back since Brian died. Two years? Three? More? Christ. And this time he wasn't staying. He had a hotel room in town and he was flying out Sunday morning.

Ardie was the one who found him, walking on down the line of trucks, wrapping him in a big hug. "Damn, West. I'm glad you're here."

"Hey, Ard. I wouldn't have not. How's everyone holding up?"

"We're doing okay. It was just a matter of time, you know? She was just a shell really since Poppa died."

Ardie kept an arm around his shoulders, slowly walking them up the lane.

"Yeah, I know." He smiled, held on. Ard looked good, damned good.

"You look tired, West. You still working too hard?"

"As hard as Lee lets me, I guess. The money's great."

Ardie nodded. "Yeah, that's what you keep saying. So things are good between you and your Lee?"

"They're okay. Lee's brilliant, you know? High-maintenance."

"High-maintenance?"

"Yeah." Lee liked things just so, liked him to be just so. It was a challenge keeping things peaceful.

"That's a good thing?"

"I... I don't know, Ard. It's a hard thing."

"Love's not supposed to be hard, West." Ardie was getting that worried older brother look.

"I never said it was love, Ardie." It was... not being alone.

"You could come home." Once a month or so, the offer was made.

"No, Ardie. I can't. Lee wouldn't like it here and you've got enough family." Hell, Lee'd thrown him out for coming down for the funeral.

Ardie nodded like he hadn't expected any other answer. "Well, I'm glad you came. You want to go in, or we could go out to the barn. See if our spot's still there?"

"Oh, let's go to the barn. I'm not here long, I have to get my visit in."

Ardie's hand squeezed his arm.

Just as they got to the barn one of Aggie's brood came running up. "Auntie Bell said to bring you this."

She had a little cooler and a small basket with food in it.

"Thanks, honey." Ardie took the stuff and gave him a grin. "She can read me like a book, that Mabel."

"That's her job, I guess." West smiled at the girl, nodded.

"Yeah. She's good at it. Come on; think we can still climb this old ladder?"

"I might. Hell, I'm a stud. You gonna let me smoke up there?"

"Hell, no. We don't want the place going up in smoke."

He rolled his eyes. "Spoilsport."

"Yep." Ardie winked and started climbing.

He swatted Ard's ass as they went. Jackass.

Ardie just laughed and then laughed some more. "Oh, man, it's freshly stocked. Looks like this isn't just ours anymore."

He looked around, grinned. "Man, we're old, Ard. We've been superseded."

"Yeah, no shit." Ardie shook his head and groaned as he got down onto the blankets. "Damn, I am getting old."

"You and me both, bud." He sat, leaned against the wall. "You and me both."

"As always, it's good to see you, West. The best. No matter why."

"Yeah, we gotta stop doing it over funerals, though."

"That's a deal, West. A damned, let's make it so deal."

He nodded, reached over, and squeezed Ard's hand. Ard was the only reason he'd made it through some of those dark, dark days.

Ard squeezed back, didn't let go. "Do you ever wish sometimes that we were still kids, West?"

"Oh, Lord, you know I do sometimes. Then I think about all the shit we had to go through, and I think, no way."

Ardie chuckled and nodded. "Yeah, I guess I didn't think of it that way."

His cell phone buzzed and he jumped, checking it. Lee. Damn. "Hey, whatcha need?"

"When are you coming home?"

"I thought you told me to leave?"

"Don't make it worse, West. When?"

"Sunday. I'll call you, I'm busy."

"You have fun playing hayseed."

"Bye, Lee." He was going to have to find another lover. Lee was... something else.

Ardie was frowning at him. "Problems at home?"

"Huh? No. No. I. It's nothing." Like he was going to bitch about Lee when Ard's mom just died.

"You sure? It didn't sound like nothing."

"Oh, it's just stuff. Nothing important. Honest. He's high maintenance. Brilliant, though."

"So you're happy?"

"What?" He wasn't looking for happy. He was just tired of sleeping alone. Happiness wasn't for him.

"I worry about you, West. I want you to be happy, yeah?"

"See? You're a good man, Ard."

"Because I want my best friend to be happy? Doesn't everyone want the people they care about to be happy? I'm just a man -- like you."

"I'm not wasting my time looking for happy, Ard. My happy is in the ground. I'm just going for what I can handle."

"West... " Ardie shook his head. "Brian wouldn't have wanted you to live like this."

"Don't, okay? Please. My visit isn't about me for once. I'm here for you."

"And I'm fine, just worried about you." Ardie raised his hands. "All right, all right. We'll just sit and be. Like old times. I'm betting the kids have some comics up here..."

West chuckled, nodded. "That sounds like more fun than I've had in years."

"Yeah? Cool."

Ardie dug around and came up with a half dozen dog-eared comic books. "Here you take this newfangled stuff. I'm going to stick to the oldies but goodies."

"That sounds about right." He got settled, flipping through, leg beside Ard's.

"God, this feels good, West."

He smiled over, nodded. "It does. It always has."

"Yeah." Ardie nodded and settled a little closer.

They got comfortable, and it was like he'd never been gone, like things were -- at least for right that second -- real again.

Too bad it couldn't last.

# Chapter Seven

Ardie took a cab from the airport straight to the hospital. He figured if he needed a hotel, he could get one later. It was late afternoon and he just hoped he hadn't missed visiting hours. It was already a day since West's call and he didn't want any other delays. He was really worried. Less by the fact that West was in the hospital, than by the fact that West had called him and asked him to come, his voice so defeated.

He hurried to the main nurses' station, overnight bag in his hand.

"Excuse me, ma'am," he said, taking his hat off. "Could you tell me where I might find West Moreland?"

She smiled, looked something up, and then asked his name. She called West's room, got permission, and then sent him up to room 224.

He had his hat in one hand, his bag in the other, and went in, calling out quietly. "West?"

"Ard?" He heard West, walked over to the second bed. West had one leg up in a cast, bandages covering one shoulder. "You came."

"Of course I came, West." He put down his bag and his hat and pulled a chair over to the bed. "What happened?"

"He got pissed off because I wanted to leave. Shot me twice."

"What? West! Jesus." He jumped up. "Where is he?"

"The police are looking. I'm sorry. I shouldn't have called. I was scared."

"The hell you shouldn't have." He settled back down, sitting on the edge of West's bed. "Why don't they have somebody posted at your door?"

He was going to have a hard time finding this guy and beating the shit out of him with the cops already looking. And of course there was the fact he hadn't a clue what the fucker looked like.

"There's security. The cops think he skipped town. He..." West sighed. "He's high maintenance."

"High maintenance? No, West, Aggie's high maintenance. This guy's an asshole who *shot* you."

"He said he loved me. Said he couldn't bear to lose me."

"That's not love, West." He took West's good hand and squeezed.

"I know. It... it hasn't been. He... It's been bad, Ard." West wouldn't meet his eyes.

"West..." God, it broke his heart. West deserved better than this. "Come home with me, West. Come be with the people who care about you."

"I... I want to."

"Well, then, come on. As soon as they let you out of here, I'm taking you home." He didn't need West to be in love with him; he did need West to be healthy, happy, whole.

"I can't. You've got kids there. A family. He'll come back." West sighed, closed his eyes. "Let's start over. H...how was your flight?"

He let West get away with it for now. Hell, he figured he had some time to work on the man. "Long. And the food? Damn. I've never missed Mabel's cooking more."

West chuckled. "Yeah. I hear you. Scary cardboard eggs."

"I bet it beats the hell out of what they feed you here," he teased.

"Yeah. They did surgery on my leg. I'm not even on real food yet." West looked old, scared, hurt. It made him ache inside.

"You will be soon enough. Bitching about the food and being stuck in bed. You remember when you broke your leg playing baseball? God, we drove your Momma crazy."

"Yeah. Other leg this time." West's eyes filled with tears and he closed them. "Where are you staying?"

"Don't know. I just got here." He squeezed West's hand, feeling damned helpless to do anything to help.

"Stay here for a while? I know he won't come back. I do. But I can't sleep."

"I'll stay until they kick me out, West. And they're going to have to be pretty damned insistent if they expect me to go before I can spring you." It would be for the best. He couldn't roam the streets of Seattle looking for someone to beat the tar out of if he was here with West.

"Thank you. You could stay at my apartment but it's a crime scene. I'm... God, Ard. Things are so utterly fucked." The tears did come then, silent and horrible.

He wanted to hug West, hold him, but West was all banged up. So he just squeezed West's hand hard and petted the lean belly. "It's going to be all right, West. Everything's going to work out just fine."

"Is the nurse coming soon? My leg hurts."

He had no clue so he leaned forward and rang the bell. "She'll be here soon, West."

"'Kay. I'm sorry, Ardie."

"For what, West?" He wasn't going to have West apologizing for getting shot.

"For everything. For this."

"Not your fault you got shot, West." He growled a little, frustrated, angry at the world for not caring for his West properly.

"I shouldn't have made him mad..."

Ardie snorted. "No, West. He shouldn't have shot you. It doesn't matter what you did. He made the choice to pick up a damned gun and use it!"

"I... I should have..."

"Come home," he teased. "Seriously, West. The only thing I can think of that would make me shoot another man is if he did something like what Lee just did to you."

West nodded, sighed. "I know. You're a decent man."

He rolled his eyes. "Yeah, yeah. A real saint to put up with you. Come on, West. I don't want to have this argument all over again. Especially not while you're down."

West nodded again, then the nurse came in and shooed him out so they could do whatever they needed to do.

He paced unhappily, wanting a doctor to tell him what the deal was, how soon he could get West out of here and home. There was no doubt in his mind he was bringing West home. Even if it was only until the man was healed.

A young, tall nurse came over, smiled at him. "Is there anything we can help you with?"

"Actually, yes, ma'am, there is. I'd like to know when I can take my friend home."

"He'll probably be released tomorrow afternoon or Monday morning." She smiled. "He's in good health and is healing well."

Oh, that was good news. The further away from here he got West, the better. "Will he be able to travel, ma'am?"

"He'll be on crutches for six to eight weeks. Need to visit a physician to get the stitches out, but medically, I would think so. You'll have to ask the doctor."

And likely the police, but he just nodded. "Thank you, ma'am, I appreciate it."

"If you need anything, let us know."

"Could I bother you for a blanket, ma'am? I'd really like to spend the night in the chair in West's room, keep an eye on him, you know?"

"No problem. The big chair unfolds into a bed. They're actually comfortable."

Well, now, he was thinking it was time the hospital back home invested in some of those. "Thank you again."

He nodded at her and went and knocked at West's door, not wanting to interrupt if they were still doing stuff to him.

The nurse let him in, West covered again, face a little pale. "We've given him a strong sedative. He needs to sleep."

Ard nodded. "I won't disturb him, I promise."

He went over to West, settling back down in the chair. "Hey, there, West. They tell me they've given you the good stuff."

"Yeah." West blinked over. "I needed you here. He's going to kill me and I thought... I thought I'd want that. But I'm not ready to go."

"You wanted to die? West..." Lord, help him he wanted to take West and shake some sense into him. "It's okay, buddy. You just get better. I'll take you home, and you'll see."

"You don't have room for me there."

"The hell we don't."

He'd build on if he had to, but with Luke gone to college and Momma dead there was plenty of room for one more.

His words made West chuckle. "God, you sound like your dad."

"Oh, now you're insulting me," he teased. He figured there were worse people in the world to sound like.

He took West's hand again, squeezed. "You sleep now, Westie-Testie. Things'll look better in the morning."

"You think?" West held on, didn't let him go. "It will. You're here."

"I am, and I'm not going anywhere without you, okay, buddy?"

West nodded, sighed softly, sinking into sleep.

Ardie sighed himself, holding West's hand until it went lax, and then he set up the chair, pulled it out into its reclining position and settled in. West was alive. He was here. The rest could wait 'til morning.

***

At first he'd thought Lee would change. Then he'd thought the screaming and the fury would stop. Then one day he'd found himself wondering if he deserved it, and he knew he had to leave.

The whole thing happened in super slow motion -- Lee's screams. The first shot to his shoulder, hot and stunning. The way it took hours to reach for the front door.

The second shot that make his legs buckle.

The way Jeannie Harolds screamed.

The way the muzzle pointed at his head.

The look in Lee's blue eyes as...

West woke up with a cry, looking around, heart pounding.

Ardie sat up with a jerk, eyes searching him out, hand taking his. "West?"

He looked at Ard, completely panicked, shaking with it. "He was going to kill me."

Ard's hand squeezed his. "But he didn't and you're alive."

"Uh-huh. God. I was scared."

"Good. Only a stupid man isn't scared when a gun's pointed at him."

He nodded, relaxing back as the room spun.

"Yeah. Yeah, missed you. Glad you're here."

Ardie petted his hand. "I'm glad, too, West. Gonna bring you home as soon as they'll let me spring you, okay?"

"What if he comes? What if they don't find him? What would I tell people?"

*Oh, I have been in a long-term relationship with a big prick.* It just didn't have a ring to it.

"That you took up with an asshole. Hell, you've got about five more to get through before you match Aggie."

"At least I just got shot, not knocked up." God, Lee should have killed him.

Ardie snorted. "Thank God, because I cannot see you pregnant. That would just be wrong."

"But marketable. Think of the money I could make selling photos."

Ardie chuckled. "I think you've got enough money, West, no need to get pregnant to make more."

"Yeah." He closed his eyes, trying to think what to do next.

"So the nurse said they were going to let you out soon. I'm bringing you home, West. And I don't want any arguments, okay? None."

"I..." He didn't know what to do, what to think. "I have to figure out what to do."

"You can figure out what to do well enough from the farm as here, West."

"I." He closed his eyes. He'd known it would come to this when he called Ard. Hell, it sounded good, to just be quiet and safe for a while. To go home.

"You know I'm right, West. It's a good place to heal, to think, to find out who you are again."

"To think? How many people live in that house, Ardie?" He smiled, teasing.

"Hell, I stopped counting after Mabel got married." Ardie gave him a wink.

"I'm not a friendly person anymore, Ard."

"I said no arguments, West. You don't have to talk to anyone. You can hide in your room, in the hayloft, whatever. I'm not leaving you here."

"No?" He laughed, shook his head. "Getting all your family home?"

Ardie nodded, eyes serious. "Yeah, that's exactly what I'm doing."

His belly just ached. "Ard."

"What?" Ardie glared at him. "You telling me you're not family anymore? Because that's bullshit."

"No. No. I just... what did I do to deserve you?"

"You were -- are -- the best friend I could ever imagine. And don't tell me you're no good, because I'm done listening to you run yourself down, West. Your last choice in boyfriends was poor, but that doesn't reflect on whether or not you're a good person."

"Yes, sir." He winked over. "Pushy old man."

Ardie laughed, smiling at him. "Oh, West. I have missed you."

"Yeah, yeah, yeah." He smiled, looking at the picture of poppies hanging on the far wall. "When can I go?"

"Nurse said it was up to the doctor, but probably today, barring that, Monday." Ardie sat forward. "You got anything at your place you want picked up before we fly out?"

"I need my computer, my files, clothes. That's it." Everything important was in a safety deposit box, kept away from Lee.

"If you tell me where everything is, I'll talk to the police, get someone to take me out there."

"Oh. I." Oh, he didn't want Ard to see the apartment -- the evidence of fighting, the broken furniture, the whole thing.

"You what, West? I don't want you having to go back if there's no reason for it."

"I don't want you to have to see. I mean, it's been bad, Ard. For awhile."

Ardie frowned. "Then why the hell didn't you go sooner?"

*Why didn't you call me?* The words echoed, unspoken, between them.

"Because I thought he'd change, at first. Because I was tired of being alone." He looked down at his hands, sighing softly. "I'm not like you, Ard. I can't just go forever without someone in my life."

"I've got plenty of people in my life, West. And so do you if you'd just look."

He looked at Ard for a long minute, then he realized it didn't matter.

Ard wouldn't understand.

Couldn't.

"I know, Ard."

"Do you?" Ard shook his head. "I should go see what it'll take to get a doctor up here to see you."

"Yeah. I'm ready to get out of here. I want my life back."

"Seems to me like that statement's a long time in coming."

"I'm not one of the kids, Ard. I work, I make good money. I got shot leaving him. Don't start."

"Sorry. I'll go find that doctor."

Ard got up and squeezed his hand and headed out.

Christ.

Just...

Christ.

*** 

The doctor made them wait to go until Monday, which had given Ardie time to go to West's place, with a police escort, and get the stuff that West needed. He boxed it all up, put West's name and the farm's address on everything, making sure they'd be found again if they got lost at the airport.

He and West had stopped at a bank on the way to the airport, West needing stuff out of his safety deposit boxes, and then they'd flown home. Business class sure was nicer than cattle class, but he didn't even want to know how much it had cost West.

And now he was trying to avoid anything remotely resembling a pothole, but he could tell the truck was not helping West out any in the comfort department.

"Almost home," he noted.

West nodded, lips tight, face grey. "I do recognize the place."

Ardie sighed. God, West had been a bitch the last couple of days and he knew the man was hurting, but it was like West was pushing him on purpose.

"I'm sorry, man. It's been a shitty few days; that's not your fault. You're going out of your way for me."

He nodded and gave West a smile. "'S'okay, West. You'll feel better soon. Some TLC in a decent bed, Mabel's food."

West nodded back. "I just want to sleep for a while, and then figure out what I need to do."

"You take as long as you need, West. Nobody's got a watch on you." Frankly, he was going to be pushing for West to stay. There had to be a way he could work from home with all that fancy computer gizmo stuff.

"Yeah." They pulled up to the house, West wincing when everybody piled out of the house. "What did you tell them?"

"That you were shot." He gave West a grin. "Us country bumpkins all figure the big cities just aren't safe -- no one knows it was Lee."

"Thank you." West lifted his chin, put his sunglasses on.

"You're welcome," he replied softly.

He got out and then went around to help West. "Don't crowd him, you don't want to knock him down."

West nodded, smiled at the kids, at Mabel. "Hey, guys."

"Say hi and then help bring West's stuff in. Upstairs." Next to his room. Lord, he was looking to torture himself, wasn't he?

West was quiet, saying hi and then slowly taking the stairs, white-knuckled and shaking at the top.

He slid his arm around West's waist and helped him into the guest room, getting him settled on the bed. "You're a very stubborn man, West."

"Who? Me? I'm just a guy." West propped his leg up on some pillows, leaned back.

He chuckled. "Just a stubborn guy." He started unpacking for West. "You want anything?"

"A glass of water. I'm going to take my pills and sleep a month."

"I doubt Mabel'll let you get away sleeping that long without trying her latest creations, but I hear you."

West grinned. "I'm not a big eater, you know? Coffee. Pizza. My life's blood."

"Oh, she makes pizza now. All sorts of fancy stuff." He headed for the door. "I'll get your water and be right back, West."

"Thanks, Ard." West curled up, eyes closing.

He hustled into the bathroom for a cup of water. He'd have to remember to keep a bottle of fresh stuff up here for West, but he didn't want to leave West hurting the length of time it would take him to go down and get some.

He was back in West's room in a minute, going through West's overnight bag for the pills.

"Just hand me the bag, man. I'll dig for them."

"I've got it, West, you just relax."

West looked at him, grinned. "You're such a nurturer, Ardie."

"Me? Nah, I'm just used to taking care of the livestock." He winked.

"Bitch."

He chuckled and came up with the bottles of pills West had. There was something to fight infection and something for the pain and then another bottle of stuff for when West was really hurting. "You okay with the regular painkillers?"

"Yeah, for now." West sighed, shifted.

"You'll be off 'em in no time, West. Good fresh air, good food, good company." He sat on the edge of the bed and handed over the pills, then the glass of water.

West looked at him. "You honestly believe that, don't you? That being here is some kind of cure?"

"For some of what ails you, yes." Maybe it wouldn't heal West's leg and shoulder any faster than anywhere else, but the man still had open wounds from Brian's death, let alone what Lee'd done to him. And Ardie firmly believed that would heal better here than anywhere else.

He got a smile, the look more than a little sad. "I hope you're right, Ard."

He nodded, took West's hand and squeezed. "Me, too, West." Because while he'd made his peace with not being with the man he loved? He refused to make peace with West being unhappy.

"Stay for a while?"

"As long as you need, West. As long as you need."

West nodded, settled. "I don't deserve you."

"Why's that, West? Because someone you loved died and you're having a hard time dealing with that?"

"This isn't about Brian."

"No? You haven't been happy since he died."

"I loved him."

"I know."

"So I'm supposed to be happy?"

"He's the one who's dead, West. Not you. And you know damned well he would not want you to spend the rest of your life just making do."

"I'm not dead. I'm lonely. I tried to find someone else. You see what happened?"

"Maybe you were just looking in the wrong places, West." God, he wasn't sure why he was going into this now.

"Maybe I deserved it."

That's what he'd been afraid of. "No one deserves to be used like that, West."

"I didn't love him." West sighed. "I didn't. I just didn't want to be alone."

"So that means you deserved it?" He shook his head. "You can say what you want, I know you're a decent person, West. You didn't deserve it."

"Maybe I did. You don't know. Maybe he knew I was fucked-up, Ard. Maybe he knew I wasn't giving him enough."

"Then he was using you from the start. West... you're something special. You deserve the best."

West chuckled. "Brian used to say no one on earth cared about me like you did. I think he was right."

Ardie looked down at his hands, feeling the blush creep into his cheeks. "You're my best friend, West. Since forever."

West nodded. "When..." He stopped short, shook his head. "I should get some sleep."

"When what, West?"

"When I woke up from the leg surgery, I just wanted to be here. With you. Home. I'm a grown man, you know? I still wanted to be home."

"Oh." He gave West a slow smile. "I think that's pretty cool, actually."

"Stay until I go to sleep?" West hadn't been able to fall asleep alone since the shooting.

He'd worry about breaking that habit later. For now he was enjoying West's needing him. "Yeah, West, I can do that."

"Thanks, man." West closed his eyes, curled around the pillows.

He pushed West's hair off his forehead. "It's gonna be okay, West."

"I know. I'll be out of your hair before you know it."

He chuckled ruefully. "That's not what I meant."

"I know." West smiled. "You would let me stay with you forever."

"I would," he said quietly. Let? In his fondest dreams it was truth.

"Thank you."

"My pleasure, West," he murmured.

West nodded, breath evening out, sleep taking him.

Ardie spent a long time watching West sleep.

***

He spent two days sleeping, then he took a shower and went back to bed for a week.

It felt good -- to not worry, to not think, to not be a real boy. Eventually, he had to get up, go to Ard's doctor, and get the stitches out. But up 'til then? He was cruising.

Ardie always seemed to be there whenever he woke up, usually awake and reading, sometimes snoring to beat the band.

He woke up the day before the stitches came out, the whole house quiet and dark. He sat up, careful to not wake Ard, and hobbled to the window. He couldn't believe he was here.

He just *couldn't*.

Ardie shifted, mumbled. "West?"

"Go back to sleep, Ard. I'm good."

"What'cha doing?"

"Looking out the window." He smiled over. "Go lay down in the bed, Ard. Get comfortable."

Ardie got up and joined him, leaning out the window. "You good, West?"

"Yeah. Getting tired of sleeping. How're you?"

"Getting tired of watching you sleep." Ardie gave him a wink.

"Yeah, I'm sorry. I just... I'm sort of lost, you know? Sleeping is easier."

"I know, West, I do." Ardie wrapped an arm around his waist. "Can't sleep forever."

He sighed and let himself lean, cheek on Ard's shoulder. "I know. I know."

"You don't have to do it alone, West. You never did."

"I know. It's been so hard. I've tried so hard, Ardie, and I just keep fucking up."

"You're just human, West. And you expect more from yourself than anyone else does."

He didn't know what to say to that. "I just don't want to be another person. I want to be something special."

"Oh, West. You *are* special."

West smiled -- he had to. No one believed in him like Ardie did. No one ever had.

"I'm just a geek, Ard."

He felt Ardie's nod. "Yep. A university graduate, hell, grad school, West. Who makes a ton of money. I don't know about Seattle, but around here, that's something else."

"I just..." He chuckled and shook his head. "Shit, I don't need to keep going over this again and again."

Ardie laughed. "It's taken you long enough to figure that out."

"Shut up, asshole." He popped Ard's thigh. "I'm a sensitive gay man, remember?"

"Ow!" Ardie was still laughing, though.

"I'll show you ow. I'll beat your ass, as soon as I'm well."

"Oh, you think you can take me? Well, I would like to see you try."

"You may be big and buff, but I? Am *quick*."

Ardie laughed. "I look forward to the day you try, West. I surely do."

"Hey! I avoided a bullet meant for my brain. I? Am superman." Either that or a total moron.

"I don't know, West, I'm not sure I make a very good Jimmie Olsen."

"You can be Lois Lane, then."

Ardie laughed. "I'm not sure she'd appreciate the comparison."

"Oh, you'd make a cute Lois." Man, if he had to run, he'd be fucked.

"You know, Westie-Testie, it seems to me that you're counting on me being a nice guy who doesn't pound on guys who are littler than me and injured to boot."

"I'm not that much littler..."

"Depends what you measure."

He blinked, mouth open in sheer shock. Then he pushed into Ard's arms, hugging hard. "Oh, sweet fuck, I've missed you."

Ard's arms wrapped around him. "Me, too, West."

"Thank you." He couldn't have done it without Ard. None of it.

"Thank you, West. For coming home."

"I..." He took a deep breath. "You're welcome, I guess. You really didn't give me a choice."

Ardie chuckled. "Are you saying I strong-armed you into coming?"

"No. I'm saying you were a pushy old man and bullied me." He almost managed to hide his smile.

"Oh, now, bullied might be a bit strong... Well..." Ardie chuckled. "Maybe not. But you needed to be home. You knew that deep down."

He nodded. "For now, at least. I need to be me again."

"Yeah." Ardie squeezed him. "Come on now. Back into bed."

"You want to join me? You can't be comfortable in the chair."

"I don't want to jostle your leg, West."

"Then sleep on the other side."

Ardie seemed to hesitate a moment. "You sure?"

"Why not? I promise not to molest you, Ard. Honest." He wasn't that big of a perv. Hell, he wasn't really a perv at all.

"No, I… I don't think you'd molest me, West. Let's go to bed."

He nodded and they settled together, just like when they were kids. Well, except for the cast and shooting and being middle-aged part. "Night, Ard."

"Night, West." Ard's hand slid along his arm, petting.

"Night, Ard." Their fingers twined together and West held on.

Just held on.

***

For the first time in days, Ardie was comfortable as he woke up.

He grunted and shifted, not terribly awake yet.

Oh. One of the kids had crawled into bed with him. He cracked open an eye, the other one flying open when he saw it was West and the memory of the night before flooded back.

West sighed, frowning, one hand on Ardie's belly, patting.

Oh, God. It was like a dream come true. Or one of the fantasies he indulged in now and then when he took himself in hand.

He shifted away, his morning wood feeling very eager.

West shifted, moved with him, sighing softly, hand petting him.

Oh, God, what did he do?

He should get up. A good and decent man would get up.

Instead he closed his eyes and pretended he was still asleep, enjoying having West lying next to him, touching him. He was going to go to hell for taking advantage of West like this, he was sure, but he was only a man and this was his fondest dream; lying with the man he loved.

West made a sweet, soft sound, relaxing against him fully.

Oh, now. Maybe this was a gift. Something to get him through the nights when West had healed and left again. He just lay there, eyes closed, breathing deeply, enjoying each moment of being so close to West. He could feel the way he eased West, the way the man's sleep deepened.

And that was one of the things that made it easier, knowing he was important in West's life, even if West didn't love him like he loved West. They stayed like that, close and warm, West sighing softly.

Finally the long black eyelashes opened, green eyes staring up at him. "Morning. Was dreaming."

"Yeah?" He cleared his throat. "Good dreams, I hope."

"Yeah. We were fishing -- nothing but you and me and a cooler. No phones, no stress, no bullshit. Just pure heaven."

He smiled. "Yeah, that sounds about right. We could go. Out back to the creek, soon as the doctor says you can hobble around on bumpy land."

"I get the stitches out today, get a lighter cast." West didn't move, stayed close.

"Well, then, we'll have to see what all he approves of. I imagine climbing into the loft will still be out," he teased.

"Damn." West chuckled, breath warm against his skin.

He grinned. "You never did do well with inactivity."

"Yeah. I need to get back to work, get back to life."

Ardie nodded, though his mood dropped a little. Was West really so eager to leave again? "You could work from here until you're back on your feet."

West nodded. "I was considering that or finding an apartment in town. I... I'm not interested in going back north."

He beamed at West -- he couldn't help himself.

"We'll find a place for you here, West. With Luke off at college and not planning on coming back, there's room enough for a bedroom and an office for you. It'd be real great to have you home for good, West. I. I've missed you a whole lot."

"I just want a place to work, to heal." West sighed. "I... I've got real money, Ard. Maybe I'll buy some land and build a little place. Maybe I'll... Oh, hell, I don't know. There's lots of options."

"Well, you can stay here until you decide. No need to rush a decision you won't be happy with." He resisted the urge to squeeze West close.

"Thanks, Ard. You take good care of things."

"I try, West. I've had lots of practice..."

"Yeah, I know." West sighed, moved away from him. "I've always said I wouldn't be one of the ones you had to deal with."

"*Deal* with? Oh, come on, West. I *want* you to stay. Don't make it sound like a chore." He'd had enough of West being down on himself.

"No? You say that because you haven't lived with me."

"Sure I have. You practically lived here while we were growing up, especially after Poppa died." Maybe the real problem was that West didn't want to live here with him. It made perfect sense; he didn't know why he hadn't thought of it before. "Of course, maybe you don't want to be stuck in a house full of kids and people."

"It's not who I wanted to be. I wanted to be metropolitan and sleek and... Shit, I don't know how to make you understand. I wanted to be one thing and it's not working and I don't know who to be now." West met his eyes. "Part of me wants to stay right here forever, part of me says that's fear talking. I mean... would you come with me? If the situation was reversed?"

"You mean if I was the one needing and you were offering me a place?" He thought on it, tried to look at it without counting in his feelings, but he couldn't, because dammit they counted for something. "Yeah. I guess I would."

West blinked, the look on his face pure surprise. "You would?"

"Why is that so surprising?"

"Because I... Because you have your family here, your life."

"Well, you said reversed. I assumed you meant all that would be gone. That you would be what family I had left, my life here... no longer a good thing." And hell, if West ever told him he loved him and wanted Ardie to go live with him in the wilds of Africa? He reckoned he'd find a way to do it.

Especially now that Mabel and Aggie and Luke had something other than the farm to keep them in food and clothes and a roof over their heads.

"Oh." West nodded and sat up, reaching for his crutches. "Man, I'm ready to get all the stitches out."

Ardie winced, feeling another opportunity to tell West how he felt slipping through his fingers. How many more would he get?

He cleared his throat. "I. Uh."

Those green eyes caught his, contacts and glasses long gone in favor of laser surgery. "Yeah, Ard?"

"I'm not asking you to stay because I don't think you don't have anywhere else to go. I'm asking you to stay because I miss you and I want you to be here where I can see you every day." It wasn't a declaration of his love or anything, but he wasn't sure he even knew how to begin to make one of those.

West smiled, leaned over and kissed his cheek. "Thank you."

He smiled, touching his cheek without even thinking about it. West's lips had been soft and warm. "You're welcome, West."

West nodded, stood. "Let's go get this damned cast changed."

He nodded and climbed on out of bed, their conversation having taken care of his little perky problem.

For now West was staying. That was enough.

***

Four weeks. Four long, long weeks and he was losing it. West couldn't bear the noise -- between the people and the kids and the animals and the phone calls? He was going crazy. He grabbed his cane, headed out to find Ard.

He'd been up all night online, talking to investors, to designers, getting back to work, getting back to himself.

He had a plan, finally. A goal. Somewhere to go.

"Ard, we need to talk."

Ardie looked up from his fertilization schedule and gave him a smile. "All right. You want to grab some Cokes?"

"Sure. I have a plan, finally."

"Oh." Ardie's smile faded a little. "All right, let's go on up to my study."

Ardie got a couple of Cokes and headed upstairs.

He got settled, looked over at Ard. "I have a plane ticket to Seattle for tomorrow."

"What? You're going? Just like that?" Ard looked... hurt, upset.

"I have to. I have things to take care of. I have to get my books, my car, deal with all the work-shit and let them know where I'm moving. I need you to help arrange a place downtown -- somewhere quiet with a window." He stretched, pulled a notebook from his pocket. "I figure it'll take me a few weeks to get back. I have a conference in L.A. in two weeks, so I'll drive there, do that, and then come home. Unless you want to take a three-week vacation?"

"Oh." The relief on Ardie's face was palpable. "I thought you meant... well, that you were going back for good." Ardie gave him a sheepish grin. "I might be able to swing the time away. But not starting tomorrow."

"Well, I'll buy you a ticket out, if you want to drive back with me."

"Can you wait a couple days, West? I need to arrange for someone to take over the chores and stuff while I'm gone."

"I could do it, Ardie." Aggie was standing in the door and she shrugged apologetically. "I was walking by and overheard you talking. I can do most of it myself, and what I can't, I know who owes us favors."

"Well, or I could go out by myself..." They hadn't caught Lee, but he couldn't live in fear. He just couldn't.

Ardie gave Aggie a look. "You sure you can do this?"

"Yeah, Ard. I figure I owe it to you anyway. And there's girls at the shop been wanting more hours, they can have 'em for a few weeks while I look after the farm."

"All right, then. Thanks, Agnes."

She nodded and gave Ardie a warm smile. "You're welcome, Bu-Pa."

Ardie turned back to him. "Looks like I'm free to come with you. I can probably swing my own ticket, though."

"No. I'll buy the ticket, Ard. Consider it a thank you."

Ard didn't say anything for a moment and then he got a wicked grin. "We going with the fancy people, West?"

"You know it, Ard. First class, all the way."

Ardie grinned. "I've got to admit, aside from worrying about you? That flight back from Seattle was very nice."

"I'm going to spoil you, old man."

Ardie chuckled. "Just getting a vacation's being spoiled enough."

"Well, I'm going to drive into town, talk to a real estate agent, get your ticket, that sort of thing." He liked seeing that smile on Ard's face, seeing the pleasure.

"So you're looking to get an office in town?"

"Yeah. It's loud here, Ard. I need somewhere I can think and work in the middle of the night without bothering anyone. I thought I'd find a little office, put a comfortable couch in it to sleep on." That's all he'd needed before.

Ardie tilted his head. "You'll be living here, though. The couch is just for those times you work late, right?"

"Well, I think we should talk about it. See if my hours are disruptive. See whether I'm a hassle." See whether they could manage.

"I'm willing to adopt a wait and see attitude, but you aren't living in an office, West."

He arched an eyebrow. "You're being pushy again."

"And you're falling back into old habits, planning on spending nights in your office on a couch. Am I just supposed to sit here and watch you work yourself to death?"

"I assume yes is the wrong answer..."

Ardie gave him a look. "Not funny, West."

He stuck his tongue out at Ard. "Bitch."

"Nope. Stud, remember?" Ardie gave him a wink.

He made a show of giving Ardie a long, slow look. "Hmm... yeah. Yeah, I can see that."

The creepy part was, he could.

Really.

Weird.

Ardie went a little red and cleared his throat, turning to his desk and pushing the papers around. "I should make a list of things for Aggie to take care of."

"Okay. Sounds like a plan..." He stood up, headed for the door. "Stud."

# Chapter Eight

Ardie felt like a little kid.

Three weeks with very few responsibilities stretched out in front of him.

Oh, Mabel and Aggie had West's cell phone number; if there was an emergency, they'd be able to find him. But barring that? He was on holiday.

And West had promised to spoil him. He'd made a joke of it, but he had to admit, he was kind of looking forward to it.

And this? Flying first class? This rocked.

His seat was nearly as comfortable as his old recliner back home, he was working on his second beer, and he thought maybe the male steward, pardon him, flight attendant, was flirting with him.

On top of that, West had brought his laptop with him, but hadn't broken it out yet.

He grinned over. "This is great, West. Thanks for inviting me along, buddy."

"I'm glad you came." West winked, leaning back. "We'll go party hardy, Ardie."

Ardie chuckled. "I'm not sure I've got the duds for partying hardy, West."

"Then we'll buy you some. Mmm... Leather pants."

He laughed out loud at that. "Leather pants. Me? Can you imagine." Oh, that was a good one.

"Oh, we'll have to. You're built, Ard. I? Look like a dork."

"You look like a racehorse. All lean lines." He shut his mouth. Vacation didn't mean his brain had to go south.

West snorted. "I'm skinny and tall and going grey, but thank you. Brian used to say I cleaned up nice."

"You don't do so bad dirty either." He gave West a wink and wondered what to do about his sudden inability to keep his mouth shut.

The air host, or flight host, or whatever it was he wanted to be called, came by and Ardie got himself another beer. "You got something to eat? This liquid lunch is going to make me sleepy."

West chuckled, "Not to mention goofy and cute."

"Goofy?" He laughed. "I'm too old to be goofy or cute, West."

"You're adorable." West chuckled, eyes laughing and at ease.

He rolled his eyes, but he was grinning, too, pleased.

"If you don't watch it, that steward'll pick you up."

"Me? Oh, no, he's just playing." And for once, Ardie was kind of playing back.

"You. And that's intense playing, Ard."

He blinked a moment. "He's not just flirting, West?" Surely the man was just flirting. Ard wasn't really an old man, but he was next to that kid.

"Lord, lord. I'm going to have to get you laid, man, if you can't tell."

Ardie felt his cheeks go red. "I haven't exactly had the practice, West."

"Well, it still works, right?"

"West!"

"What? It's an honest question."

"I'm not *that* old. Geesh, West. Of course it works." He took a long sip of his beer.

"Good to know." West chuckled, sipping a Bloody Mary. Bastard.

"So, where are we staying?" he asked, changing the subject before it got even more out of hand.

"Well, we could stay at my old place, but I thought we'd have more fun in a ritzy hotel."

"Yeah? Like with a mini-bar and bathrobes and stuff?" That sounded like fun.

"Yeah. In-room hot tub. Room service. Great view. HBO on the tube. All the perks."

"I don't think I've ever been in a hot tub, West." He had to admit, West knew how to have fun.

"Then it's about time, Ard. It's about damned time."

Yeah, he thought maybe West was right.
***

It was harder to be in Seattle than he thought it would be.

Thank God Ard was there.

It wasn't as if he needed protecting or anything, but it was nice to have someone to show the city to. Someone to laugh with. Someone to talk to.

Ard made things right.

They were sharing a room at the Meridian, Ardie just drinking it all in, from the hot tub, to the room service, to the big old bath towels. Tonight they were having dinner at a seafood place, Ardie wearing the lobster bib and wielding his mallet, though the food wasn't in front of them yet.

He hadn't laughed so long and hard in fifteen years. "Oh, you? Are adorable. Utterly."

"Oh, now don't you be laughing at me -- I'm sticking you with the bill for this very expensive plastic bib I've got."

"Oh, ho! Is that it?" He'd ordered steak and shrimp, was looking forward to it, too.

"Yep." Ardie gave him a wink. "You know I've never had lobster before? Looks like this is a trip of firsts."

"It's a little challenging, but I bet you can manage."

"Well, shucks now, I don't know, West. Does it involve math?" Ardie had let his accent go thick, words slow.

"Oh, don't make me beat you, Ardie Bodine." He'd helped Ard through all those classes, knew Ardie could do it.

"I thought you said you weren't into that strange shit."

West stopped, blinked, then started laughing hard. "You bitch."

"Nope," Ardie said with a grin. "Stud."

They were still laughing as their food arrived and Ardie's eyes just about bugged out at the sight of the huge lobster on his plate.

West just rolled, cackling madly. "Oh, sweet Christ. Your face..."

"I thought the mallet was a *joke*. And this thing is *huge*." Ardie grinned at him and hefted his mallet, giving the lobster a good solid crack.

They cackled and he helped Ard work through the process of getting the lobster opened and edible.

God, this was hilarious.

By the time they were done, they'd laughed themselves out, eaten a ton, and Ardie's hands and face were a mess. "Thank God for the bib," Ardie said in all seriousness.

West nodded, grinning over, warm and happy inside. "You know it. We couldn't go dancing if you were a mess."

"I'm still not sure about this dancing thing, West. I've never really done more than a few rounds in the front room with the girls. And Luke, to teach him how." Ardie wiped his hands and mouth on his napkin. "Well, there was that time you took me to that party back when you were in college. I have never forgotten those Martin and Wilma fellas. Gals. Whatever."

"Marty is living in San Francisco now. Wilma died a few years ago -- testicular cancer, can you believe it?"

"Oh, that's a shame. They seemed nice enough."

West nodded. He'd lost touch with almost everyone that wasn't from work. "We'll go somewhere queer-friendly. It'll be nice."

"I did enjoy two-stepping with you the last time." Ardie gave him a smile that was almost... shy.

"I did, too." He remembered being surprised that Ard could dance, could move so well. "You'll have to take it easy on me and my old leg."

Ardie chuckled. "Oh, I don't think you'll have any trouble keeping up with this old man."

"Yeah, I mean that three months you have on me? Vast amounts of time." Dork.

"It is! At least I remember it used to be." Ardie gave him a wink.

"Yeah, yeah, yeah." He chuckled, wiped his mouth. "You want dessert now or later?"

"Oh, let's save it for later. I'm truly stuffed."

"Yeah, me, too." He handed his credit card to the pretty little blond waiter and stretched. "We should go walk it off."

"Anything you want, West." Ardie gave him a grin. "You know I'm having the time of my life? Thank you."

"It's about time we just relaxed together, Ard. We both deserve it."

He signed the slip, then stood, waiting for Ardie to grab their coats. They did deserve this. Both of them.

Ardie passed West's coat over and nodded as he slipped his own on. "Yeah, buddy, we do. Makes me feel young and carefree again, all this. You know how long it's been since I felt this way?" Ardie chuckled and shook his head. "Shit, I'm not sure I ever did."

He nodded. "It was like this with Brian, sometimes, but we were working so hard, building our careers. It seems like a shame now, but at the time it didn't."

Ardie reached out and squeezed his arm. "Funny how what's important changes, isn't it?"

"Yeah." He chuckled. "And how some of what's important doesn't."

"Yeah." Ardie gave him a smile, eyes soft and serious. And happy.

"Come on, Ard. Let's go play."

"Lead on, West. I'm right behind you."

He hooked his arm in Ard's, nodded. "Right beside."

Right where Ard seemed to belong.

***

Ard ordered himself another beer and looked around the bar with wide eyes. He was in way over his head.

Way over.

He'd been okay as long as West was nearby, but someone had asked West to dance and he'd grinned and waved his friend off.

They'd only had a single drink; they were working up to the dancing when the guy had come up and asked West to join him on the floor. Damn, it was good seeing West up and about and having fun. Still, he was pleased when the song ended and West shook his head at the guy he was with and headed back toward Ardie.

West smiled at him, eyes dancing. "Come on, stud. Dance with me."

"I just got a beer," he pointed out. He put it down, though, and took West into his arms, grinning at his friend. Oh, this was nice. Really nice.

West nodded, stepped close as they moved together. It felt good, moving together, the music. West was warm and pliant in his arms. Real good. Better than real good.

West rested a cheek against his shoulder. "This okay?"

"Hell, yeah." It was better than okay, it was damned good.

As one song slid into another, he let his own head drop, cheek resting on the top of West's head.

West didn't tense, didn't do anything but relax further. "Oh, I've missed dancing."

"I can see why. This is nice."

His eyes drifted closed and they started to just sort of sway together. He could almost believe it was just the two of them.

West's arms circled his waist, fingers moving slowly, petting him.

Oh.

Oh, this was a gift. An amazing, wonderful gift. It would be so easy to just whisper the words in his heart, but he didn't. West didn't need that kind of pressure right now, didn't need to do anything but enjoy this.

One dance turned into another and another.

Then another.

Finally West looked up. "Your beer's getting warm."

"Is it?" He smiled down. "I guess I can live with that."

West grinned, eyes shining. "Yeah? Then we could just keep dancing."

"We could."

He tightened his arm around West's waist. He could just do this all night.

"Cool." West looked... happy. At peace. Sort of like how he felt, just at this moment.

He wished they could freeze time, right here.

They danced until midnight, until West was favoring his injured leg, leaning heavy into him.

"You want to sit and have a beer or something, West?" Give that leg a bit of a rest before they headed back to their hotel.

"I do, yeah. Man, I haven't had so much fun in forever. You... you can dance with me anytime."

"Just you wait, I'll turn the front room into a dance hall, and we'll have dancing every Saturday night."

He kept his arm around West's waist, leading him to the bar and helping him get settled. "We'll have a couple beers," he told the bartender.

"Oh, that? Sounds fun." West nodded. "We'll tell everyone it's exercise."

He chuckled. "The kids'll roll their eyes, but I bet you Mabel and Billy'll join us. Maybe we'll even get Aggie to stay home now and then." He gave West a wink.

"So long as you dance with me."

"Well, that's the point of the whole exercise, isn't it?" He grinned. Oh, he was flirting, wasn't he? Just smiling and teasing. With West. It felt damned good.

"You know it. I only dance with the best."

"Oh, I bet you've had some fine partners, West."

"I have. That doesn't make you any less for me."

He dipped his head. "Thank you."

Their beer arrived and he took a long drink, trying to come up with something to extend the evening.

A tap came to his shoulder, a tall blond smiling at him. "Excuse me, would you like to dance?"

"Me?" He couldn't have been more surprised if the man had asked him to go home with him. "I'm. Um."

"Go on. You'll never know what a shitty dancer I am if you don't try." West winked, nodded.

He grinned at West and tried not to panic. "All right."

He stood, feeling awkward, and put his arm around the man's waist like he was West.

"Hi. I'm Rick. Nice to meet you." He got a smile, a nod.

"Howdy, Rick. I'm Ardie. Likewise."

Once they started dancing, he didn't feel so awkward. Oh, it wasn't easy and right like dancing with West was, but it was nice just the same.

The song ended and they danced another, Rick smiling at him. "You... can I buy you a drink after this song?"

He tried not to panic. He was so not ready for this and he was going to kick West's ass.

"Well. I'm kind of with my friend, but you could join us."

"Sure, if your friend wouldn't mind."

"I'm sure he won't." Well, he hadn't a clue really, but he didn't know what else to say.

He took a breath and brought Rick back over to West. "Um, West, this here is Rick. Rick -- West."

"Hi, Rick." West shook Rick's hand, smiled.

Rick nodded, sat down close to him. "What are you drinking, Ardie?"

"Just a beer, thanks." He shot West a 'help me' look, the one he used to use when Annie Lester caught him in the halls at school.

West smiled, scooted closer to him, one hand sliding in his lap. "My Ard's a fabulous dancer, isn't he?"

Oh, lord.

He swallowed hard, managed not to make the surprised noise that was trying to get out. His prick got real interested, too, and he couldn't exactly move away, now could he.

This had never been West's answer to the help me look with Annie.

He liked this version of help better.

"He is. Are you two a thing?"

"Have been for years." West turned his face, lips sliding against his, warm and easy.

His mouth opened on a gasp, lips pressing against West's. Oh. Oh, it was nothing like he'd imagined. Soft and warm, simple and just... devastatingly easy.

West's eyes went wide, shocked, then the kiss deepened, West's tongue sliding against his own. The moan came from somewhere deep inside him and his tongue moved with West's, following West's lead.

West's hand came up, cupped his jaw. He heard a soft chuckle. "Christ, you two. Get a room or invite me to join in."

He pulled back, shaken to the core, unable to take his eyes off West. "Sorry," he murmured. "I--"

"Yeah. Time to go. Sorry, uh... guy." West stood up, held out his hand. "Come on?"

He nodded and took West's hand and let himself be led out without a look backward. It was rude, and he might come to regret that, but he was floating, shaking, just... spellbound. West didn't say a word, just held his hand, led him down the street toward the hotel. West's hand was warm, felt so good in his, and he had to remind himself that the kiss had just been a way to save him from Rick.

Still, he was feeling more than a little giddy, and he was happy for the cold weather, hoping it would cool his jets a little before they got back to the hotel room they shared.

\*\*\*

West was stunned.
Fucking stunned.

He'd loved the dancing -- felt good and all warm and shit -- but that kiss?

Sweet lord.

He hadn't expected it to be good.

He hadn't expected it to be anything.

It was.

God.

Just, God.

He looked over at Ardie, blinking, stunned.

Okay. Hotel. Elevator. Room.

Room with a bed.

No. Bad idea.

Room with a suite. A couch. That's right. Couch.

Hot tub.

Christ.

"How's your leg?" Ardie asked him as they got to their room. His friend's eyes were wide, bright.

"Fine. It's good." He couldn't stop looking at Ard, just *looking*.

"Good." Ardie nodded and gave him a smile. It started friendly and grew warmer and then Ardie kind of blushed a little and ducked his head.

"I... The kiss... It was... I didn't know it would be so..." Good? Big? Right? Sweet?

"I know you did it to rescue me from Rick."

"I started for that, yeah." He wasn't going to lie, wasn't going to let Ard believe he was faking it.

"Started?" Ardie's eyes slowly lifted, met his.

"Yeah. Yeah, but... that's not why it, uh, kept on."

Something flared in Ard's eyes. "Yeah?"

"Yeah." God, he wanted to do it again.

"I." Ard looked down at his hands and then back up, that slow smile coming back. "It was my first kiss. Are they all that good?"

"Not as a rule, but there's no reason we can't try and see." He stepped forward, breath catching in his chest.

"Oh." Ard's eyes went to his lips, stayed there. One hand wrapped around his waist like they were about to start dancing again and Ard bent, touching their lips together.

He pressed closer, just one step, close enough to feel Ard's heat. Then his lips parted, making the offer, letting Ard in. Ard's tongue slid against his lower lip, slid away, and then came back again, hesitant and sweet.

It was enough to make him whimper, to make his heart pound. Damn.

A moan vibrated between them, coming from Ard, just like back in the bar, and Ardie's tongue pushed in further. He nodded, meeting Ard's eyes, arms reaching up to circle Ardie's neck. Yes. Please. Ard's other arm went around him and he was tugged closer, the kiss going on.

Oh, sweet Jesus. What was he doing?

His fingers were in Ardie's hair, tongue sliding and playing and it was good. So good. Ardie pulled him even closer and he could feel the heat of Ardie's cock against his lower belly, hot and hard. He pushed against that heat, moaning low. Oh, hell. Yes.

Ardie's hands held him tight, the kiss getting harder, more intense. West just let himself go, let himself push close, rub.

Ardie fed moans and whimpers into his mouth, a shudder going through the long body. "West..."

"Yeah, Ard? You want to stop?"

"What? No!" Ardie was a little breathless, eyes so wide, pupils just huge. "I. No. Not unless you want to."

"Thank God." He grinned, pushed back into Ard's arms, kissing deep and hard.

Ardie made a muffled noise and then he was kissing back, tongue sliding along West's, arms wrapping tight around him. He didn't think about it, didn't worry, just felt. Ard was broad, strong, hot against him.

One hand slid back to his ass, cupping it, holding him close, while the other slid slowly up and down his spine, fingers warm through the material of his shirt. He just sort of melted, pressing as close as he could, hips rocking and sliding against Ard.

Shudders shook Ard as they rubbed together, sounds feeding into his mouth, Ard's tongue sliding with his own. God, these breath-stealing kisses could just go on forever.

"So good." He panted, kissing the corner of Ard's mouth, the dimple in the strong chin. "So good, Ard."

"Uh-huh." Ard nodded and hugged him closer. "Like nothing ever."

"Mmm..." He brushed their lips together, tongue teasing, gaze caught in the pleasure in Ard's eyes.

Ard whimpered, hands tight on his ass and back. "Think maybe I need to sit. Or lie down."

"We can do that. The bed?"

Ardie nodded, panting, squeezing him a moment before letting him go and taking his hand. He leaned his head on Ard's shoulder and followed. Went easy, too.

Went so easy.

\*\*\*

Ardie sat on the edge of the bed, West coming down with him, still sorta in his arms and he just turned a bit and wow, there was West wrapped in his arms again.

He couldn't quite believe this was happening. They were kissing and stuff and he was so hard he hurt, only it felt good, too, because he was here with West and as long as they didn't stop, he was going to. They were going to. Oh. Yeah.

He didn't know what to say so he just found West's lips again and they were so soft and it felt so good, so much better than he could have ever imagined, and he wondered why he hadn't done this sooner. If all it took was kissing West, why hadn't he just *done* that ages ago?

They settled with West pressed against him, hard and warm and relaxed and so fine. So fine moaning and purring and rocking into him. It was like all his best fantasies had been granted, only it was so much better in real life than in any fantasy. Sure, he was worried about doing something wrong and about West suddenly deciding this wasn't a good idea, but everything else? Oh.

This could just be the end of time and he'd be a happy, happy man.

Kissing West was like... a ball of warm and good and he felt it right down into his fingers and his toes. He felt it in his cock, too. Lord help him, he wanted to come so badly, everything just throbbing and making his pants seem so tight.

"I want... You want to... I mean, I want to touch, Ard." West pulled at his shirt.

Oh, God, yes.

He nodded and helped West, undoing his buttons with fingers that were not trembling too badly.

"I didn't know. I mean, I never really thought, but it's good. It's so good." West was murmuring, lips and hands hot on his chest.

"I thought about it a lot," he admitted, eyes rolling, soft gasps leaving him at West's touches. "It's better."

"Why didn't you say?" West's lips found one of his nipples, pulling just lightly.

"It's complicated." And he didn't really want to go into it right now, because he couldn't think when West did that, could only buck and whimper, that little girly sound coming from him.

"Mmm..." West purred, fingers working his belt open, his jeans. Oh, God. Oh.

He knew he should get West naked, too. Hell, he wanted to touch West, but he was just... Oh, God, West was going to touch him. Another shudder went through him and his cock just throbbed so hard and any second now it was all going to be over.

West's fingers wrapped around him, sweet and hot, pumping him.

"Oh, God! West, I'm gonna!" He reached out, holding onto West's arms, body just shaking -- he was fixing to fly right apart.

"It's okay. I've got you, Ard. I've got you."

He whimpered, forehead resting against West's, mouth searching. As their lips pressed together, his whole body bucked and he shot all over West's hand.

"Mmm... so hot. So hot." West just purred, the sound amazing and sexy and better than anything he could imagine.

He kissed West, coming down slowly and not really coming down all that far. "That was. Oh, wow."

"Yeah. Yeah. I... Wow." West kept touching, fingers hot and hard on his cock, just exploring.

He moaned, cock staying hard, balls tight, still wanting. He'd never come and still needed before, never like this. "West. I want to touch you, too."

West nodded, face lifting for a kiss, green eyes looking like he'd only imagined. Looking at him. "Please."

He pressed their lips together, caught in West's eyes, in the sensations that kept him flying, floating. His hands weren't exactly steady as he undid West's buttons, the backs of his fingers brushing against warm skin. West helped, let him see, let him touch the soft, warm skin.

There was a scar where the bullet had gone through West's shoulder, and he was skinny, not quite count your ribs skinny, but more bones and skin than much else. Two flat little nipples that drew Ardie's fingers.

"Oh." West smiled, cock sliding on his thigh, so hard in the expensive slacks.

He swallowed and gave West a grin. Damn, this was good. He was like a kid in a candy store, except he was no kid and West was way better than any candy. He focused on West's pants, pretty sure he wasn't going to be able to manage the button and the zipper without watching what he was doing.

West chuckled, fingers in his hair, petting him almost. "You look like Christmas morning."

He grinned. "I feel like Christmas morning. And I just got the best present ever."

"Flatterer." West chuckled, nuzzled him.

"No, just the truth. I've been. God, I've imagined this a million times, West." His fingers were trembling as he opened West's slacks. "Oh, God."

"Touch me?" West's hips rose up, letting him slide those slacks down.

"Hell, yes, just you try and stop me." He reached out, fingers sliding along West's cock. It was hot, silky, so hard.

"Mmm..." West's mouth opened, the look all hot and hungry. "Ard. That's good."

"Yeah? You'll have to... have to tell me if I do something wrong." He wrapped his hand around West's cock, tugging, squeezing.

"I will. You won't. Damn, Ard. I can't believe we're... And it's so big..." West licked his throat, groaning, panting.

"Too good not to be real."

He just kept stroking West's cock, his other hand sliding over the warm skin of West's chest. He wanted to take his time, to explore, to learn everything there was about West that he didn't know, but there was so much, he just didn't know where to start.

"Yeah. So good." West's hips started to move, slide that long cock in his hand. "Like dancing."

He laughed, but it was, they just fit together and moved together like they were made for it. He squeezed his hand around West's cock, free hand tilting West's head back up so he could press kisses to swollen lips.

"Oh, Ard." West's eyes were stunned, hungry, desperate.

He moved his hand faster, knowing it was what he liked, figuring it couldn't be much different for West. One of West's legs landed atop his, hips thrusting hard now, snapping. His own cock jerked, the back of his hand rubbing against it now, and he moaned, tongue pushing into West's mouth.

Oh, God. West starting sucking his tongue, making him wonder how that mouth would feel farther south. His whole body went a little tight at the thought, hand squeezing West's cock hard.

West grunted, heat spreading over his hand, just like that.

"Damn."

A shudder moved through him and he kept hold of West's cock, hand on West's back, not willing to let go yet. He didn't want this to be over. Not by a long shot.

"Oh. Oh, shit. Ard. That. Lord." West blinked at him, so close he could see all the colors in West's eyes.

He smiled, the feelings inside him so huge he just had to let them out. "Love you, West."

West blinked, reached up and cupped his jaw. "How long?"

He rubbed against West's hand. Damn, it felt good to finally say it, to finally tell West the truth. "For just about ever, feels like."

"Oh." West smiled, eyes stunned, searching his. "Why didn't you tell me?"

"Well. I didn't know you were gay, too. And when I found out you were already with someone. And you had plans and I had to stay and run the farm. It just never seemed like the right time, West. I wasn't going to try and get between you and someone else when you were dating and then it didn't seem right to say, 'Oh, sorry it didn't work out between you and that guy, and by the way I love you'."

"I never knew." West looked stunned. "God, you must think I'm an idiot."

"To be honest, West? I've been kind of thinking I'm the idiot for not saying something." He shrugged. "It just never seemed to be the right time. I sure hope this was."

West nodded, cupped his jaw. "I... You surprised me. *We* surprised me. You're my best friend; I wasn't supposed to melt when I kissed you."

He felt the smile grow from deep inside him. "Kissing me made you melt?" God, he was grinning like an idiot.

"Kissing you was like touching a live wire, Ard. I..." West chuckled, grinned, blushed dark.

He reached out and touched West's cheek, realized suddenly his other hand was still wrapped tight around West's cock. He found he didn't really want to let go.

"You what?" he asked, feeling the heat pouring from West's cheek, making it almost as hot as West's cock.

"I've never felt anything like that. Ever."

"Really? Never? Not even." He closed his mouth. He wasn't sure he wanted to be bringing Brian up at the moment. This was about them.

"Not even." West chuckled, the sound bittersweet. "We were so young. Things are... different now."

He wrapped West in a hug. "I don't ever want to let go," he admitted.

West lifted his face, smiled. "Then hold on."

\*\*\*

They spent the rest of the early morning hours talking and it was sort of weird -- mingling best friend with lover -- but sort of not. West didn't worry about it, tried not to think about it. It was still Ard, still his best friend for twenty-five years. It was still good.

They dozed off at dawn, both of them facing each other, watching each other. Ardie's eyes were so full of wonder, of awe and happiness, that smile still on his face as his eyes drifted closed.

It was late when he woke back up, the sun low in the sky. He felt good, warm. Settled.

It was vaguely terrifying.

Ardie was still asleep, one arm wrapped around his waist, fingers curled and warm. Ardie looked about ten years younger. He reached out, slowly explored Ardie's face, stroking the faint lines, the planes and valleys.

Ardie smiled, nuzzling into his touch before his eyes slowly blinked open. "West." Oh, that smile was something else. "It wasn't a dream."

"No. No, Ard. It wasn't." It wasn't.

"Can I kiss you again?" Ardie asked softly.

"I probably have morning breath..." He nodded, grinned, nose touching Ard's.

Ardie chuckled. "Me, too. You want me to go brush my teeth?"

"No. I bet we manage okay." He kissed the corner of Ard's mouth.

"Okay." Ardie turned his head just a touch, bringing their lips fully together, hand around his waist dragging him up against Ard's warmth. Heat. The morning wood definitely seemed to be in working order.

He moaned, lips parting, letting Ard in. His skin was tingling, warm, heated. He could feel everything -- the sheets under his side, the air on his shoulder, the way Ard's hair tickled his belly. Ard's tongue slipped in, exploring him carefully, fingers beginning to move on his skin, too.

"Oh." He scooted a little bit closer, legs tangling with Ard's.

Ard gasped, hips starting to move, sliding their cocks together. "Oh, West."

"Uh-huh." He nodded, needing. Hungry for it like he hadn't been in years, since Brian.

Ard's tongue tangled with his, hips moving frantically. He groaned, arched, watching Ard's eyes, staring.

"God, West." Ard pushed him over, rubbing against him.

He moaned, spread, arching up. "Feels good. Don't stop."

"Won't." Ard's tongue slid back into his mouth, body moving fast and hard. "Oh, God. Oh."

"Uh-huh." He grabbed Ard's ass, tugged them together.

"West!" Ardie's eyes went wide and he thrust hard, heat spraying between them.

That was... yeah. He ducked his head, panting against Ard's shoulder.

"Oh. Oh, West." Ard kissed his neck, moaning softly.

"Uh-huh." West nodded, so hard, just aching for more.

Ard's hand slid down to touch his cock. "You didn't come yet."

"Was busy watching you."

Ardie blushed. "Me? Couldn't be that much to look at."

He chuckled, shook his head. "Don't argue with me, Ard. We're *busy*."

"Okay. No arguing when we're busy. You'll have to tell me all the rules, West, I'm new at this." Ard gave him a wink, hand sliding slowly on him.

West laughed, pushing into the touch just like they'd been doing it forever. Ardie's hand felt so fine.

"Is this good, West?" Ardie looked so earnest, wanting to make him feel good.

"Yes. God, yes. You have amazing hands, Ard."

"Me? You sure?" He got another wink, a wide, happy smile on Ardie's face.

"Ardie. Teasing your lover when he's hard and needing is mean..." He chuckled, hips bucking towards Ard's hand.

"You see? You'd better tell me *all* the rules." Ardie was almost giggling, eyes just dancing.

"Rule number one. Orgasms are good. Real good."

"I think I already knew that one." Ardie grinned and tugged on him. Cock getting hard again, rubbing on him.

"Rule number two. Kissing. Good."

Ardie nodded vigorously. "Yes. It is."

Ardie's lips found his. He groaned, tongue moving in time with his hips, heat flooding him. Ardie moaned, hips pushing that long cock against his thigh. He wrapped his legs around Ard's hips, holding on, rocking them together.

"God. West." Ardie's weight was just right.

"Yeah. Don't stop, okay." He reached up, petted Ardie's face.

Ardie shook his head and nuzzled. "Don't want to stop, West."

"Oh. Oh, good. This... this is just right." Their eyes met; caught. "Just right, Ard."

"Yeah. It is." Ardie kept pushing, cock sliding alongside his, leaving a wet trail on his belly.

"Need you." The words escaped him, pushed out before he could even think. Oh. Oh, God.

Ardie beamed down at him. "Love you."

"I... Ard." He tugged Ardie down, shooting hard, surprising himself, just bucking into Ard's hand.

Ardie's eyes went wide and he pushed a few more times, adding more spunk between them.

"Damn. I. Good morning." He shivered, stole a kiss. "I mean afternoon. Evening."

"Hi." Ardie smiled and nuzzled against him a minute before sliding slightly to the side and just kind of wrapping around him.

"Ardie." He relaxed, leaned, sort of basked in them.

"This... is something else, West." Ardie was gazing at him, one hand sliding through his hair, pushing it off his face.

"Yeah." God this was... Unreal.

Fascinating.

Scary.

Perfect.

Ardie's lips nuzzled his ear, hands running along his skin. It felt like almost like Ardie was reading him. Like Braille or something.

He almost purred, just relaxing into the touch. "You're... I never thought you'd be so sensual."

"Well, I don't know about sensual, West, but I've got a lot of years to catch up on."

"Were you waiting for me?"

There was a pause and then Ardie nodded. "Yeah, I guess I was."

Something in him twinged a little. "I might not be worth it."

Ardie laughed. "Shut up, West."

"What, are you making rule three?"

Ardie nodded. "I am. I don't want to hear anyone running down my lover. Not even you."

He grinned, shook his head. "Kiss me, Ard."

Kiss me and make everything go away again.

\*\*\*

Sleeping, room service, making love. Ardie didn't want to ever leave the hotel room. He felt like the luckiest man on earth. He'd just been granted his only true wish.

Ardie put down his spoon, happily stuffed. "So what's rule number four, West?" he asked.

"Hmm? Umm... Rule four is you have to share your whipped cream." West looked relaxed, melty, happy.

"I can probably manage that." He slid his finger through the whipped cream in his dessert and reached across the table.

Those green eyes flared and, oh, sweet Lord...

West leaned over, took his finger in those lips and started sucking. Oh, God. His cock just throbbed and his lips parted. It was... Oh, God. West's head just bobbed, taking his finger in deeper and deeper.

"West." God, was that his voice, all hoarse and strained just from West's mouth on his finger?

"Mmmhmm." Those eyes were just twinkling.

"That's..." Sinful.

And giving him ideas.

He swallowed, hips pushing against the air without him even thinking about it.

West nodded, tongue flicking his fingertip.

Oh, God, he was gonna come if West kept that up.

"You want... I could suck you off, Ard. You want my mouth?"

"Shit." He closed his mouth on a whimper and nodded. God, yes, he did.

West slid down between his legs, spread them, worked his jeans open. His hands curled around the armrests on his chair, frozen, watching. Not quite believing.

"This okay, Ard?"

He reached out and touched West's cheek. "Yeah. I just... it's something else, West." He just didn't have the words.

Then West's mouth dropped over his cock, so hot, so good.

"Shit!" His hips bucked and then he collapsed back into his chair, shaking.

West purred, fingers sliding against his balls, stroking, rolling them. He gasped for breath, damned near crying, it was so damned good.

He didn't want to come, he wanted this to go on, he wanted to watch West's face as West's mouth slid on his cock, but it was so good, too good. "Oh, West. Gonna."

West moaned, took him in deep, eyes watching him close. He just lost it, the pleasure too big to hold in. His hands went to West's head, needing to touch as he shot deep inside West's mouth. West took him in, took him deep, drank every drop, then cleaned his cock.

He stroked West's face, melted and shaken. "Thank you," he whispered.

West kissed the tip of his cock. "Thank you, Ard."

"For what?"

"For twenty-five years."

"Oh." God, his heart was just going to burst right open. "I'll give you twenty-five more. And then another twenty-five after that."

"Yeah? I'll take you up on that."

"You'd better." He smiled, still stroking West's face. "I think that should be rule number five. That was. I don't think my legs work." He chuckled.

West grinned. "Tell me about it. I'm down here, I don't know if I can get up."

"But nobody sucked your brains out of your dick."

He held his hands out for West, more than happy to pull the man up onto his lap. West took his hands, settled close, close enough that he could see the way those lips were swollen -- from him.

He leaned forward and licked at them. They were hot and as he slipped his tongue into West's mouth, he realized that was himself he could taste there.

Oh, God.

West moaned and leaned in, lips parted, open for him, letting him taste. When he'd imagined this, he'd never known West would be so relaxed, so peaceful against him. Their kisses were long and languid, like they had all the time in the world, which he guessed they kind of did.

He was happy to leave tomorrow and the details of work and the farm and where they'd live and what they'd tell the family pushed away.

"You doing okay, Ard? You happy?" West nibbled on his chin, his jaw. "Having a good vacation?"

"You have to ask? Damn, West, I'm having the best vacation *ever*. What about you?"

"It's a little chilly for my taste, but all-in-all? Not bad." West chuckled, licked him. "Not bad at all."

"I'm not keeping you warm enough?" He tried for affronted, but he just couldn't get rid of the smile that kind of lived in his voice the last couple of days. Since this vacation had started, actually, but it had definitely gotten worse. Better. Whatever.

"Mmm... more snuggling. In fact, I hear? Skin to skin's the warmest."

"That sounds good. I imagine you'd like me to do that mouth thing to you, too." He slid his hand down to West's crotch.

"Only if you want, Ard. I'm not gonna push things." Oh, West was hard.

"But if I wanted. You'd like it?" Though, really, he couldn't see how anyone in their right mind wouldn't.

"There's not a man alive that doesn't."

"Can we do it in the bed? And you'll tell me if I'm not doing it right, right?" He was suddenly unaccountably nervous, like this was his audition or something. What if he hated it? What if he was no good at it?

"Ard. Man. Chill." West leaned in, kissed him good and hard until he couldn't think about anything.

His arms went around West and he hummed, moaned, lost himself happily in the kisses. West rubbed against his belly, the touch of West's tongue against his so hot. He slid one hand around and into West's pants, grabbing that sweet little ass.

It didn't take long before West was bucking, moving sure and steady against him.

He slipped his free hand between them, pulling open West's button and undoing his zipper. A bit of a push down of West's jeans and a tug up of his shirt and sweater and West was rubbing skin on his skin. God, the man was hot. Cock like a brand against his belly and it was sexy and good.

"Mmm..." West leaned down, forehead on his shoulder, panting. "Close."

"Yeah? Good. I like the way you smell."

"Uh-huh..." Heat sprayed against him, West moaning low.

He squeezed West close and tipped his head, licking at West's lips. "God. You're... it's good."

West just nodded, blinking up at him. He took a kiss, eyes locked on West's. He could spend the rest of his life just looking, just holding. Just being here.

With West.

"Mmm... what rule are we on?"

"Um... six?" Fuck if he knew for sure.

"Mmm... have we covered post-orgasm snuggles?"

"I don't know, West, but they sound like they're either a lot of fun or very twisted." He gave West a wink.

West's laughter filled the hotel room, just echoed.

Well, now, he loved that sound -- always had.

He held West close, holding onto the laughter.

# Chapter Nine

It was incredibly hard, going to the old apartment, walking up the stairs. It probably was reasonable and normal and okay, but it was hard. The key still fit in the lock, the door patched with putty, showing where Lee had... Yeah.

Things were cleaned up some, quiet, the blood and broken glass gone.

Okay. Okay. He just needed to pack his books and his leftover crap and go.

Go.

Okay.

Ardie came up with a couple of boxes in his arms. "You want these anywhere in particular, or should I just follow you with 'em and you can dump stuff into them?"

"Whatever. It doesn't matter. I'm easy."

"Funny, you don't look easy. You look tense." Ardie put the boxes down and came over, hands dropping to his shoulders and rubbing. "You okay?"

"Yeah. I mean, I don't know. Maybe? This is deeply fucked-up."

"Well, you're just getting the stuff that's important to you and then someone can come in and clean the place out and you'll sell it, right? It shouldn't be a long job."

The impromptu massage turned into a hug, Ard's body long and strong behind him. Warm and solid.

"Yeah. Yeah. Just my shit and then zoom." Every creak made him jump, shiver. "Over there. The first shot was over there."

Ard squeezed him. "He's not here now, West. And I am. He won't hurt you again."

"Yeah. Yeah. Just... is the door locked?"

Ardie went over and locked it. "Yes. Come on. Let's get what you need."

"Okay." He started packing his books, the few odds and ends he had. "Is there anything in the kitchen that Mabel would want?"

"Are you kidding? She's got every single utensil, pot, and kitchen gadget known to man. She gets this wholesale catalogue once every few months? You should hear her -- you'd think she was having amazing sex the way she carries on about that thing."

He chuckled, packing the coffee maker and such for his office. "There's a visual I didn't need."

Ardie chuckled. "Prude."

"Bitch." He grinned right back.

"Nope. Stud. Which I think I've more than proved."

He grinned. "Now, now. You haven't jumped my ass once."

"Well, not for lack of thinking about it." Ardie gave him a sheepish look. "You keep distracting me with kisses and hand jobs and blow jobs."

He grinned over. "So you're blaming the horny gay guy now?"

"Is that me or you, I forget."

"You, apparently, are the senile gay focus of the horny gay guy's... horniness."

Ardie laughed and then stopped. "Wait a minute. Are you calling me senile?"

He hid his face behind a book. "Did you forget already?"

"Westonbury Moreland, you better start running."

"You don't know this place as well as I do, Ardie-Pardie..."

"But I'm bigger than you, Westie-Testie."

"I'm way faster." Or he used to be.

"Yeah, but I've got to figure you're too horny to be fast. Maybe if you're lucky, when I catch you I won't remember why I was chasing you to start with."

He thought about that for a second, missing the fact that Ard was moving closer.

Ardie laughed and caught him up around his waist. "I think you're the one going senile, West. You forget you were supposed to run?"

"No. I didn't want to miss this." He lifted his face for a kiss.

"Oh." Ardie smiled and bent to give him that kiss, lips warm and firm, tongue sliding into his mouth.

He groaned, pushing right in, cuddling into Ard's heat. Ardie's hands slid, one grabbing his ass, the other pushing into his shirt and spreading on his back, warm and solid.

"God." He closed his eyes, ignoring the apartment and focusing on Ard's lips.

Ard pulled him close, tongue sliding deep. "Taste so good."

"Mmm..." Ard felt so good, so hot against him. Lord, they shouldn't be doing this here.

Ardie leaned back against his desk, sending something flying to the floor with a crash. "Shit. Oops."

West started chuckling. "This place is cursed."

Ardie grinned at him and nodded. "Yeah. Let's get your stuff and go. I can think of better things to do than hang out here."

"You and me both." He smiled a little, looking around. He had never been happy here. Never.

Ardie's hand slid on his back. "You never have to see the place again, West. It's not home."

"No. It never was. Never."

Ardie's chin rested on his shoulder. "You were lost. You're found now, yeah?"

"Yeah. Yeah, I guess I am." Either found or insane -- either one worked.

"Well, come on, then." Ardie kissed the side of his mouth and gave him a quick squeeze and then bent to pick up the books he'd knocked off the table. "You want these?"

"I do. Do you think I should ship the big desk and comfy couch for my new office?"

Ardie looked around. "You're loaded, right? I think you should trash the whole deal and start new."

"Yeah? The desk was nice, but we can find anoth... Did you hear something?"

Ardie shook his head. "Come on, you're freaking yourself out, West. Time to get what you want and get out."

"I can't... I need my books, I think..."

Ardie looked around, eyes narrowed and then nodded. "Okay. Let's go. We'll call someone and arrange to have it all shipped home and you can go through the boxes there." Ardie took his hand and headed for the door.

"Ard..." He followed, sort of stunned, sort of surprised.

"What? You don't need to be here; it's obviously making you unhappy. You need to learn to leave stuff that makes you unhappy behind."

"You think?" His fingers twined with Ardie's, held on. "You don't make me unhappy."

"Well, thank God for that." Ardie squeezed his hand and leaned forward to kiss him.

"You're my best friend, West. I mean, more now, but first there's that."

"Yeah. Yeah. That's... forever."

Ardie nodded and gave him a soft smile. "I hope the rest is, too."

"I..." He stopped, looking up at Ard. "I don't know about that, Ard. I'm... I'm scared to want forever."

"Because of Brian?"

"Yeah. Because I wanted forever so badly and then he was gone. Do you have any idea what'll happen to me if I lose you?"

"I know. I know. I'm not going anywhere, okay?" Ardie hugged him hard.

"I want to die first. I know that's selfish, but it's true."

"Just don't be too eager to go, West."

"I'm not. I wasn't, even when Lee... I mean, he was going to kill me, and I didn't want to go."

"Good. I'm not eager to be left on my own either, you know. But I've let too many years pass by without telling you how I felt to not just hold on for as long as I can now and want it to be forever."

"Take me out of here, Ard. I don't want to be here anymore."

"Whatever you want, West."

Ard's arm went around his waist, his friend, his... lover walking him out.

***

Ard arranged for someone to go in and pack up all of West's stuff at the apartment and ship all the books and papers to the farm. Everything else was to be sold, along with the apartment itself.

He called for room service steaks and then he got the hot tub full. "Hey, West. Gonna come show me how this thing works?"

West wandered in, naked, at ease in his own skin. "There oughta be a button or a switch or something."

He just kind of stared, still not really used to the idea that he *could* without having West deck him or giving away his secret.

"Am I okay?" West turned in a circle, looking.

He grinned a little sheepishly. "More than. Just admiring."

"Oh!" West turned bright red, the color actually going with the black and white decor of the fancy-pants bathroom.

He chuckled. "Don't tell me you're shy, Westie-Testie."

"Hey, you seem fond of my testes, Ardie-Pardie."

Now it was his turn to blush. "Yeah, I guess I am."

"Now, now. Don't tell me you're shy, Ard."

"Come over here. It's easier not being shy with my tongue in your mouth."

West chuckled, headed over. "You're getting spoiled."

"I am." He nodded, smiling as their lips met.

Oh, he loved that, acres of naked skin, all for him. His fingers were in love with West's skin, all hot and smooth. He explored. God, would he ever get tired of exploring West?

He hoped not.

"In the tub, Ard." West grinned, wriggling a little.

"Pervert."

"You have a point?"

He chuckled. "And so do you." He rubbed his hard cock against West's belly.

"Mmmm..." West's eyes lit up, fingers teasing his prick.

"Oh..." He shivered. He wasn't sure he was ever going to get used to this. He didn't know if he wanted to -- he liked it being so special, so good.

"You okay, Ard? This okay?"

He nodded. "It still feels a little unreal, a little like the most amazing fantasy ever."

"Does that mean you're not going to let me sleep with you when we get home?"

"What? Why wouldn't I?" He held West a little closer, a little tighter. He hadn't really been thinking beyond Seattle, but he'd assumed whatever they did, they'd do it together.

"You said it was a fantasy. They don't tend to come all the way home." West offered him a kiss. "You'll have to explain. I'd understand if you didn't want to."

"Well, Mabel knows how I feel. She'll help." He shook his head; he couldn't imagine hiding West away like a dirty secret, no matter how long it was going to be. "I'm not letting you go, West. If this is a fantasy? I'm not waking up back to reality."

"Oh." West searched his eyes, the look stunned, shocked. "I've never been someone's one and only before."

"Sure you have. You just didn't know it." He gave West a wink.

"Right." West blushed. "I can't believe it. That you don't hate me."

"Hate you? Why would I hate you?"

"For not knowing. For not noticing. For being a clueless fuck."

"Well, I could have said something. And I never did. Maybe you hate me."

West chuckled, leaned into him. "Not even a little."

"No?" He grinned and kissed West's nose. "Good."

"Yeah. Real good." West chuckled, kissed his chin.

"We're wasting hot water, West. Tub time."

"You go first and I'll sit in your lap."

He grinned and blushed a little. "You're going to get more than just my lap..."

"Promise?" West licked his jaw.

He looked down and grinned. "Oh, yeah. I think that's a pretty safe promise."

"Excellent. You first." West looked... wicked.

He got into the tub, settling comfortably, groaning a little at the way the hot water just made everything feel right and relaxed. Well, almost everything. West slid in, warm and slick in his arms, the added weight making his ass slip on the wet marble.

He chuckled, arms wrapping around West's waist, the water making his skin slick. "Oh... This is nice, West." His prick was snugged up against West's ass, West's back warm against his chest.

"Uh-huh." West's ass started rocking, sliding against his cock.

He groaned and his head went back, hitting the edge of the tub. "West."

"Uh-huh?" West groaned, shivered.

"This is... it's good. God. I knew it would be. Just never *so* good. I never thought..." He just hadn't known.

"Never? Never once thought about my ass?"

He laughed and bit West's shoulder. West's skin tasted of salt and something good that he thought was just West. "I thought about it, just not enough."

West chuckled, leaned forward, that ass just offered to him.

He swallowed hard, hands moving to slide along the softly rounded buttocks. "Do you... Can I... I want to make love to you, West."

"Oh. Oh, I'd... I'd like that, Ard. I haven't... I mean, it's not something I did a lot. Only Brian."

"We don't have to," he murmured. He wouldn't push West, not for anything. He was more than happy with the stuff they'd done.

"I want to. I want to feel you inside me." Oh, God. West sounded... Amazing.

"Yes. Yes, please." He leaned forward to kiss West's spine, hands massaging West's ass.

"Mmm... Good. Touch me." West's hips rocked. "Touch me."

"As long as you'll let me," he murmured. He slid one hand around, finding West's cock hard, hot.

"You promised me forever."

"I did." He smiled, eyes closing as he rested his cheek against West's back, his one hand sliding along West's cock, the other moving, fingers finding West's crack.

"Oh. That's right. Touch me." West rocked, moving against his touch.

He did, fingers exploring, finding West's hole, the smooth, smooth skin beyond it, the back of West's balls. The water moved against his fingers, against West's balls, West's thighs. West's breath seemed to have synched up with the splash of water against the side of the tub, his own was panting from him.

West leaned, rested against one edge of the tub. He knew the basic mechanics of what they were going to do and so he took a deep breath, made himself calm down a little and then pushed at West's hole with one finger.

"Mmm... That's it, Ard. Love me."

"I do, West. I do."

His finger pushed right into West's body and he moaned at the tightness, the heat. God. That was going to be something else around his cock.

"Oh. Oh. I can feel you. Damn." West squeezed him, hips jerking.

"West! Oh." Oh, God. It was going to be... "It's really tight. *You're* really tight."

"Uh-huh. More, Ard. Please."

"You sure, West? I don't want to hurt you." He hadn't expected things to be so tight.

"I'm sure. I am." That sweet ass pushed back against him.

"Okay. Don't let me hurt you." He took a deep breath and worked a second finger in, moaning at the way it felt.

"Mmm..." Oh, that didn't sound pained, not at all.

He moved his fingers in and out and kind of focused on the tile across the tub, because his cock was just aching, hard as anything, his prick rubbing the back of West's leg.

"You... Damn. Soon, Ard, okay? I need it."

"Me you mean? Okay. Do I need something? Like a condom or some lube or something?"

"There's oil, Ard. The condom's up to you, how safe you feel."

"Well, I ain't never done this before, West. I guess I'm clean." He reached for one of the little hotel bottles on the lip of the tub.

"I meant me, Ard. I haven't done this in a while, but I've done other stuff."

He bit his lip, pondering. "I don't want to use a condom, West."

"I don't have anything, Ard. I swear it." West looked back at him. "I never trusted Lee enough to even suck him without protection."

"I don't want to live like that with you," he murmured, hand sliding on West's cheek, thumb rubbing West's lips. "I trust you."

West's eyes -- those green-green eyes -- met his. "I love you, Ard. You know that, don't you?"

He knew, hell, they'd been best friends since the second grade, but hearing West say it now gave it new meaning. "I love you, too, West."

"I know." West turned, settled in his lap, facing him. "I know. Want to see your face."

He nodded, hands sliding around West's waist. "I'd like that."

He got one hand around his cock, rubbing it beneath West, searching for that tiny little hole. God, even that felt amazing. West slowly sank down onto him, lips parting as tight heat surrounded him.

"Oh, God." It felt... shit, like nothing ever, like his cock was just going to explode inside that tightness. The heat was unbelievable. It felt... so good.

"Yeah. Yeah, I. It's good, Ard. Don't stop."

In and in went his cock until West was sitting in his lap, Ard's cock buried deep, and God. He swallowed hard. "Just sit tight a moment, West. If I move I'm gonna come."

"Okay. Okay. Kiss me?" West leaned in, watching him, staring at him.

He stared back, mouth merging with West's, tongue pushing deep. West moaned, body clenching around his, almost rippling. It was insane.

"Oh. Gotta move." He didn't think he was gonna last long, but he just had to move, West's body demanding it from him. He pulled back a little and then pushed in again, moving instinctively and God!

He cried out, eyes flying to meet West's.

"That's it. Love me. Fuck." West looked stunned, happy. Beautiful and looking at *him*.

He swallowed, emotion so thick inside him, he could hardly breathe.

He wrapped his hands around West's waist, holding on, moving West a little to help with the in and out thing, and damn, it was just better than anything ought to be.

He found a rhythm, something that made West's nostrils flare and made those eyes stay dark and happy, something that made his own toes curl, and he just stayed with it, the pressure and pleasure making his balls ache.

"Yes..." The water seemed to cling onto West's skin as they moved, as West bounced.

As West rode him.

It was all too much, the water splashing against them, against the tub, West's body, so tight around his prick, the sensations sliding through him. But most of all there was West's eyes, looking into him, everything West felt laid out in them and he cried out, cock throbbing inside the tight sheath of West's body.

West groaned, just watching him, looking at him. "You're beautiful."

"Me?" He felt the blush rise up from his belly, making even the backs of his ears hot. "You're lust-addled." He winked, and congratulated himself on having the presence of mind to wrap his hand around West's cock.

"No. No, Ard. You are." West arched, throat working, body tight on his prick.

Him, beautiful. His chuckle was rough, that emotion still thick inside him, and he watched West as he continued to pull on West's hard cock.

"Want... Oh, so sweet, Ard..." West's eyes rolled, entire body flushing dark.

West was the beautiful one, pleasure making him shine. Ardie pulled harder on West's cock, feeling the heat and velvet of it against his palm.

"Love..." Heat sprayed, West's ass squeezing him, milking his cock.

He shivered, something like aftershocks going through him at the sensation. The water soon cleaned up his hand and West's cock, but he kept holding on, just not ready for the moment to be over yet.

"Thank you. I... Wow." West leaned into him, kissing nice and slow.

"Mmmhmm." Wow was right.

The kiss was lovely and hot and lazy and good. Just the thing to cap off what they'd done.

"Was it as good as you thought?"

"Hell, West, I don't have a good enough imagination to have thought *that*. Not like that. It was all just... kind of theoretical." He grinned and took a hard kiss. "It was good for you, too, wasn't it?"

"Mmmhmm." West looked... melty.

His cock got a good, hard squeeze, then West cuddled closer.

"God. West. I'm too old for you to be making me hard again." He wrapped his arms around West, just holding on, the warm water like a blanket around them, the air a little humid and steamy.

"You're making up for lost time."

He chuckled. "Maybe I am at that."

"Happy? Too hot in here?" West's hands moved restlessly, aimlessly.

"I'm pretty easy, West. Whatever you want." He took one of West's hands and brought it to his mouth, kissing the palm. "Whatever you want."

"You'll do just fine."

"Oh." He smiled and kissed West's palm again and then placed it on over his heart. "I know the feeling, West. I know the feeling."

West's fingers curled against his chest, holding on.

Holding him.

Yeah, he knew that feeling and it was just fine.

\*\*\*

They'd gotten dressed before supper'd come; Ard pulling on a T-shirt and his jeans, West just the jeans. It had been a distracting way to eat, but fun. And he couldn't seem to stop smiling. Good lord and butter, he was turning into a sap in his old age.

"Do we have to do anything with the cart?" he asked when they were both stuffed on steaks and potatoes and a couple of beers. "Or call them or something?"

Just as he asked, there was a knock at the door and Ardie laughed. "Well, there's my answer."

Grinning, he made his way to the door, wishing he'd thought to ask West how much to tip the bellboy.

Hands landed on him as soon as he got the door open, a tall blond in a black trench coat trying hard to move him, slam him against the wall. What the fuck?

"Hey!" Ardie yelled and grabbed the guy's wrists, tugged them off him, shoving back, trying to get the guy back out the door.

"You fucking two-timing prick! Sleeping around on me!"

Ardie heard West gasp, heard something fall to the floor and break. "Lee?"

Lee? This was the Lee that had tried to kill his West?

Ardie kind of growled. He could feel the sound building and building in him as every hurt that West had ever suffered at the hands of one boyfriend or another coalesced into the man in front of him.

He let go of Lee's wrists, pulled back his right arm, and decked the man as hard as he could.

Lee's head rocked back, slamming against the doorframe, but to his credit, the man didn't go down, just swung right back and caught Ard's jaw.

"I'm calling the cops, Lee! They'll put your ass in jail!" Shit, West could *scream*.

Ardie didn't spend any time worrying about rubbing his jaw, he just set his feet and punched Lee in the gut with one hand and right in the middle of his chest with the other.

There was a grim satisfaction in this, in getting a bit of his own back for West.

The man groaned, scrabbling at his waistband. Oh, fuck no. Not gonna shoot *anybody* else, goddamnit. Not while he was on watch.

He sent a good solid punch at Lee's jaw, aiming to knock the man right out before that gun could come into play.

Lee grunted and staggered back a few steps, swaying dangerously. West was at the door then, trying to push it closed.

"He's got a gun, West. That door's not going to stop bullets."

He pushed West aside and went after Lee again. Damn the man for not having a glass jaw, anyway. He got another hit in to the man's face and pushed him up hard against the hall wall, arm across the man's throat. "You are going to leave West alone now, you hear me? He doesn't want anything to do with you, asshole!"

"He's *mine*." Lee bared his teeth as three big-assed security guards came rushing up.

Ardie felt another of those growls building in his chest and he let it out. With those security guards about to break up the party he only had one more shot to make sure Lee understood, very clearly, that West was with him now. Not Lee, not anyone else.

"*Mine*," he shot back. "You got that, you lowlife pond scum? He's *mine*."

He got in a couple more hits, could feel his knuckles splitting on Lee's teeth. Pretty boy wasn't going to be very pretty anymore. Not without some dental work.

"Come on, come on. Break it up. What's going on now?" The security guards were all business, pulling him away and keeping them apart.

West came out, talking fast and hard until the police showed up. Hell, once they got the gun away from that fucker, they all started to be a lot nicer to him.

The adrenaline was making the pain in his knuckles and jaw little more than a blip, and he just wanted to drag West back to his room and kick everyone else out.

Lee was in handcuffs, and man, that felt good, knowing Lee was going to get what was coming to him for shooting West.

West was giving a statement and then the detective from before - Sarah or Sally or Susan or something - came in and took over.

Ardie was trying not to growl, knew it wouldn't help his case any, but damn it, he wanted these people gone.

He went over to West and wrapped his arm around West's waist, holding on. Let the detectives think what they wanted. "Can't this wait until morning?"

"You'll need to come in to the station in the morning, give a statement. This one? Is coming with us."

Ardie nodded, growled out, "Good." He hoped they threw away the damned key. "You make sure he doesn't wave his gun at anyone else."

Finally - *finally* - they all left, and it was him and West and a locked door. West sat there, looking at him, white as a sheet. "You... you okay, Ard?"

He looked at his knuckles, skin broken and bloody. Then he looked back at West. "Yeah, West. I imagine I am."

He opened his arms.

\*\*\*

Lee.
Fuck.
He.
Damn.

West felt like he was going to shake apart. Either that or he was going to start screaming.

Screaming actually sounded kind of doable.

Ardie's face was buried in his throat, arms wrapped around him. "What about you, West? You okay?"

"Yes? No? Shit." He couldn't catch his breath. "I don't know, Ard. He could've hurt you."

"I think he was aiming to finish what he started with you that night. He had a gun, West." Ardie's arms tightened around him. "He can't hurt you now."

"How did he know we were here? He." West blinked. Oh, God. "In the apartment. We heard him. In the apartment."

He was going to puke.

Ardie nodded slowly. "That makes sense. You know, though, there is a good thing about this, West. He's caught now. He's not still out there. And you weren't hurt."

"No. Did he hurt you?" West pulled back, eyes searching his face. "Are you okay?"

Ardie moved his jaw back and forth and met West's gaze. "He didn't hurt me, West." Ardie's hands came up, fingers sliding over his cheeks. "And he didn't hurt you. He didn't hurt you."

"How could he? Christ, Ardie. You kicked his ass." West chuckled, remembering how fucking huge Ardie'd looked.

Ardie grinned. "I sure as hell did. Felt damned good, West, after what that asshole did to you."

"My hero." West actually laughed, some of the tension fading away. "Shit, Ardie. No one's done that for me since second grade."

"I guess I just like being your hero." Ardie was beaming at him, smiling wide.

His stud.

"You do a good job, Ardie-Pardie. A real good job."

"Yes, sir, Westie-Testie." Ardie pulled him in close again, sobering. "Not going to let anyone else hurt you, West. They'll have to come through me first."

"You... You know that's not why. Why I want you."

Ardie's eyes widened. "Never occurred to me, West."

"Oh." He grinned, relaxed a little. "Good."

"I know why you want me, Westie-Testie." Ardie's eyes were twinkling.

"Yep. Your money. I'm totally in this for the money."

See him. See him keep a straight face.

Ardie didn't, though, chuckling away. "Oh, if that's the truth, West, you're in for a world of disappointment."

"I doubt it. I know what I'm getting into."

He so did, down deep.

# Chapter Ten

West was nervous.

No, scared.

Petrified.

It was one thing to be Ard's lover in the city, on the road, but in Ard's house?

With the kids and the family and everything.

Christ.

He sat in his car, watching Ard open the gate, trying not freak the fuck out.

Ard got back into the car, hand moving to sit on his thigh, where it had been the bulk of their trip. "You're already family, West. We're just making it official."

"You sure you want to do this, love? I don't want to screw up your life."

"Stop the car, West."

"Huh?" He hit the brakes, half-scared Ard was going to tell him to go now that everything was set to come back.

Ardie's fingers went beneath his chin and turned his face to look into Ard's. "I love you, West. I've been wishing most of my life to introduce you as my lover. I'm not going to change my mind now that I can."

He was given a long kiss, Ardie's tongue pushing into his mouth. "Now, let's get home and give them the good news."

"Oh. Okay." It was a dazed and beaming man that pulled into the farm.

The whole brood came out to meet them and Mabel took one look at her brother and crowed. "It's about damned time, Maynard Bodine."

"About time what?" asked Agnes, looking from Mabel to Ardie to him.

Ard chuckled and slipped an arm around his waist. "Me and West are together."

Aggie's mouth dropped open. "As in fucking?"

"Aggie! Keep a civil tongue in your mouth while the kids are up and about!" Ardie frowned at her. But then he chuckled, and who could blame him, because she looked about as shocked as could be.

"Well, I'm sorry, Ard. I thought you were going to die a virgin. I never realized... "

"Aggie." West looked over, grinned, cheeks on fire. "Shut up, and tell your brother congratulations."

"Yeah. Christ. Congratulations, Ardie. What the hell you going to tell the church ladies?"

"That at least you're not pregnant again." Ardie looked like nothing was going to phase him just now and that hand around his waist stayed there.

"Bu-Pa? What does it mean?" asked Alice.

"It means me and West are going to be together like your Aunt Mabel and Uncle Billy."

"You gonna have a wedding?"

"I don't know." Ardie turned to him. "You want a ceremony or party or something, West? To mark the occasion?"

"I just want to be home for a while, Ard." Please. He still wasn't used to there being so many people.

Ardie nodded and smiled. "Yeah, West is right. Maybe to mark a year or something. For now, let's just get settled." He nodded to the kids. "Go get our bags and put them in my room, okay?"

"Okay, Bu-Pa!" They ran over to the car, arguing about who got to carry what.

West met Mabel's eyes, smiled. "You cool with this, Bell?"

She laughed and grinned at him. "Are you kidding? I've been telling Ardie off for not saying anything to you for *years*. It's about time he brought you home for real."

"It all happened fast. So fast, once it happened."

She laughed. "Oh, I'm glad you added that last bit, West, because I would say that was the longest courtship in history."

Ardie'd gone red. "Can't be a courtship if only one party knows, Mabel."

"Exactly, you big lug."

West chuckled, shook his head. "I needed time, Bell. I needed to know it was time to come home."

"See? I was biding my time until it was the right time." Ardie's arm felt good around his waist, right.

Mabel snorted, the sound so like Ardie. "You were just too scared, Bu-Pa."

Ardie was beet red now, eyes on the porch. "Yeah, maybe."

Mabel chuckled and leaned up to kiss her brother's cheek. "Well, I'm real glad you finally said something." Her eyes narrowed suddenly and she looked over at him. "He did *say* something, right? Or did you guess?"

"I kissed him. Then I sort of kissed him again."

Mabel bopped Ardie on the arm. "You didn't tell him! You big goof."

"Hush now, Mabel -- our friendship was more important. I didn't want to put any pressure on West. Don't you have something to cook or bake?" Ardie's hand had tightened on his waist. "I'm taking my lover upstairs now."

His cheeks went red and hot, but he nodded. They'd waited forever to lie together in a bed of their own.

Ardie's suddenly mischievous look should have warned him, the man looking suddenly fifteen again, and damn, Ardie could move fast when he wanted to. Ardie bent and picked him up, one arm beneath his shoulder and one beneath his knees, carrying him over the threshold, laughing and happy.

His laughter was swallowed in Ard's kiss, West getting lost in it, just like that.

Ardie took him upstairs, kissing him all the way, breathless by the time he was put down in Ardie's room. He got a grin, Ardie looking sheepish but happy. "I couldn't resist."

"You spoil me. I'm not going to know how to manage, being so happy."

Ardie chuckled. "I imagine you'll figure something out. Probably work too hard and make me come to your office and drag you home or something."

"Oh, okay. That's a good plan." He grinned, looked around. "You going to let me live in here with you?"

"I was hoping you would, West." Ardie looked around the room. It was simply decorated, walls dark blue, a couple of early football days trophies on one shelf, a bunch of pictures of him and Ardie from second grade on up to one from when he was visiting with Brian. There was a blue toned quilt on the double bed, a heavy dresser with a television on it, and a big easy chair.

"We could redecorate. Mabel's been after me to fix it up and you could have a room that was your very own, too, but I was kind of hoping you'd want to stay here with me nights."

"I'd like that. I hate sleeping alone." And his Ard was like a little furnace.

"Good." Ardie beamed down at him. "We should test the bed out. Make sure you like it."

"We should. We've waited a long time to make love here."

Ardie nodded and brought their lips together, tongue parting his gently.

When the kiss ended Ardie was smiling, leading him toward the bed. "I've done a lot of fantasizing in this bed."

"What have you wanted most?" If he could, he'd give it to Ard.

"You've already pretty much fulfilled every fantasy I could ever have. It's been... well, the last few weeks have been unbelievable."

"Yeah. It's been... damn." West grinned up, smiling. "I still can't believe it."

"I can. Now. Having you here. In this room. That somehow..." Ardie shrugged and kissed him, softly, sweetly. "This makes it all real."

"Make love to me, Ard?"

He got a slow, sweet smile. "That would be my pleasure, West. My total pleasure."

Ardie's mouth met his again, those brown eyes gazing at him, smiling at him.

He leaned into Ard, hands sliding up into the thick soft hair. "Love."

"Yes." Ardie nodded and smiled again, fingers working his shirt out of his jeans. "God, I love touching you."

"Yeah, you're like... magic, Ard."

Ardie grinned at him. "I'm just a farmer, West. Oh, I shouldn't be telling you I'm not magic, should I?" Ardie chuckled and tugged him down onto the bed. "I don't mean to ruin your sweet talk, West. You just take me by surprise."

"You're more than just a farmer to me. You're..." His eyes filled, surprising him.

"West! Shit, what's the matter?"

"Nothing. I'm... You've been my whole life and I didn't even know it."

"Nothing to cry about, West. We're here together now." Ard's big hands slid on him, warm and solid, caring for him.

"I know. I'm just being silly. Let's screw around."

Ardie laughed. "Okay, West."

He nodded, hid his face in Ard's shoulder, and got to work on buttons and zippers and shit. Ard returned the favor, fingers baring him and then exploring him. Ard's touches were always so careful, searching out the things that he liked, what made him hot. And Ard always remembered, using everything he learned to send him higher the next time.

He moaned, arched, shoulders sliding on the comforter, on Ard's bed.

"God, you're sexy," murmured Ard. "Make me want so much."

"Just an old geek."

"Careful now, I'm still older than you, remember." Ardie's eyes were just dancing.

"Older and buffer." He grinned up. "Is buffer a word?"

"Yep. It's what bald guys do to their heads. They buffer them."

He started laughing, deep down, just tickled. God, he loved this man.

Ardie laughed and held him close. "I always have loved the way you laugh at my silly jokes."

"You've always made me happy, Ard. Always."

"Good. That's why I was put on this earth."

He drew Ard down, took another kiss. "Glad I finally figured it out."

"Me, too."

Ardie rolled onto him, letting him feel Ard's weight and heat. The kiss was long and breathtaking, Ardie moaning into his mouth. His leg wrapped around Ard, held them tight together while Ard rocked against him, hot and solid.

"Good. More. Love." His lips found a smooth bit of skin, fastened on.

Ard gasped, rolling them to the side, hand sliding to his ass. Oh, somebody liked that. He sucked harder, rocking harder, letting Ard feel it.

"West... oh." A stretch, and the sound of a drawer opening, and then Ard's slick finger slid into him, opening him carefully.

"Mmmhmm." Hell, yes. Oh. And also more.

"So hot and tight. God, this is... good. So good."

In and out, Ard's finger worked him, stretched him, slicked him.

"More. Please, Ard. More." He was flying, burning.

A second finger pushed in alongside the first, Ardie moaning, rubbing their fronts hard together.

"Oh. Oh, yeah. So hot." He couldn't help moaning and riding that touch.

"I want you." Ardie kissed him deep. "Need you, West."

"Yours." He looked up into those eyes, just lost. "Come on, now. Take me."

Ardie rolled him onto his back again, settling between his spread legs, cock nudging at his hole.

He groaned, leaned up to lick Ard's lips. "In your bed."

A shudder moved through Ard and then that hard cock sank into him. Ardie's eyes never left his.

It was just right, all of it, the creak of the bed, the blankets beneath them, all of it. Ardie moved slowly, sliding in and out, pleasure making his cheeks flush with color.

"I love you."

"Yeah. Yeah, Ard." He nodded, grinned, just loving it.

Ardie smiled back, moving faster, harder, breath starting to come short and uneven.

"Yours." West reached down, started pumping his cock, hand moving furiously.

"God." Ardie moved faster, moans turning into whimpers, needy and urgent.

He groaned, shoulders rolling as he bucked, needing to shoot, to come.

"Soon," whimpered Ardie, his movements becoming jerky.

"Uh-huh. Now, love. Now." He came, orgasm sliding right up his spine.

Ardie cried out, pushing into him a couple more times before heat shot into him.

"Love..." He watched the pleasure, the need in Ard's face.

Ardie's eyes drifted closed and then open again, smiling down at him. "Oh. That was... good. It's all so good." Ardie's weight dropped down gently onto him.

He nodded. Good. Good and home.

Ardie kissed his forehead. "You feel right in my bed."

"Our bed."

That smile was something else and all his. "Yeah. Ours. Welcome home, West."

"Thank you, Ard. Been a long road to get back here. A long, long road."

"I'm glad you kept following it, West. I needed you."

He lifted his face for a kiss. "You were waiting here for me."

Ardie's tongue slid across his lips and then he was given a real kiss. "I was."

He slid his hand into Ard's, fingers twining, tangling together, his soul at rest. At peace.

Home.
End.

Printed in the United States
86850LV00008B/1/A